My Name Is America

The Journal of Biddy Owens

The Negro Leagues

by Walter Dean Myers

Scholastic Inc. New York

Birmingham, Alabama
1948

May 1

Baseball. Man, I love this game! This was probably the most exciting day of my whole life! All the exhibition games were good, and the working out and getting into shape, but there's nothing like opening day.

People were taking pictures of the team getting ready, some pictures of us in front of the team bus, even me putting the bats and bases in the equipment bags. Charlie Rudd, the bus driver, helped me get the equipment bags on the bus, and I could see that he was happy, too. Some of the Negro businessmen were around, talking to the guys, slapping them on their backs like we were on the way to a party. One photographer had us all kneel on one knee in front of the bus, making sure that he could see BIRMINGHAM BLACK BARONS behind us.

We had met at Bob's Savoy Café, and when Piper Davis told us it was time to go to the stadium I was as jumpy as a cat. Piper, who played second base and managed the team, said I looked like a tadpole in a frying pan.

I didn't care — I was starting the season with the Black Barons, and you could not ask for more than that. Mr. Hayes, who owned the team, had got a bunch of cars together for the opening day, and we piled into them for the drive to Rickwood Field. When we did that, people watching us started cheering. Boy, it sure made me feel good. The Parker High School band struck up a tune and started high-stepping ahead of the cars to lead the procession. Yes!

So there I went, Biddy Owens, equipment manager, scorekeeper, errand boy, and sometimes right fielder, which I really want to play.

Our opening game was against the Cleveland Buckeyes, and they had changed into their uniforms down at Rush's, the best Colored hotel in Birmingham. When the Birmingham crowd saw them drive up in their bus, they gave them a cheer, too.

The drive to Rickwood Field took thirty minutes. Rickwood holds about 12,000 people, and it was already crowded. People were buying lemonade and sodas, and you could smell the roasted peanuts and hot dogs.

"It is truly beautiful." That's what Piper said as we started carrying the equipment into the Barons' dugout.

When I put the bats in the rack I was not thinking this was the Negro Leagues or anything like that. I was just looking at how green the grass was and how the blue sky looked like it was going to stretch on forever over the whole world just for us. I was mostly the equipment manager, but Piper knew that I wanted to be a regular with the team. He told me that if I put on a couple of pounds I would get the chance.

I'm tall enough — five foot ten inches tall — but I only weigh 135 pounds. Looks like nothing I do is going to put more weight on me right away. Daddy says the weight will come with age (I am seventeen), and Aunt Jack says I'm skinny because the good Lord don't want me to be no ballplayer. Aunt Jack blames a lot of things on the Lord.

The Parker band started up the national anthem at exactly five-thirty, and the game started right after. That is a funny time to start a game, because the sky is still light enough to see but changing color. That is why they turned the lights on. Right off you could see that the Barons were going to outplay the Buckeyes. Everybody was on their game and they were making plays in the field like they were back at Alabama State on the practice field. Just nothing to it at all. It was a few innings into the game when Ed Steele, our left fielder, jumped on a fastball and hit a blast out toward left field. Ooo-wee! It looked to me like the whole world was holding its breath as that ball went flying. At first you could see it good, white against the deep blue sky, then it turned dark for a few seconds, and then gold as the lights caught it on the way down into the stands. They stopped the game right then and there, and this is what Ed got for hitting the first home run of the season:

Two chicken dinners from Porter's Club
One chicken dinner from the Brown Derby Café
A diamond-studded watch
Five dollars from the Davenport and Harris Funeral
 Home
Another five dollars from the Orange Bowl Drink
 Stand
And two dinners from Bob Reed's Blue Bird Inn

The Barons went on and won the game 11 to 2. Everybody went home happy.

May 2

The little hand of the clock on top the icebox was already just about on twelve, and I knew I was supposed to be at Rickwood by one-thirty. Aunt Jack was making lunch, like she always did after church on Sundays, and taking her good, sweet time about it. Daddy was sitting in his chair nursing a cup of leftover coffee, and Mama and Rachel were upstairs changing out of their church clothes.

Aunt Jack asked me how many games they were going to play today, and I told her they always played double-headers on Sundays. Daddy asked me if Sam Jethroe was still playing center field for the Buckeyes, and I told him yes. I went on talking about Jethroe, and right in the middle of it Aunt Jack asked me who visited Daniel in the lion's den. When I didn't remember, she started in about me knowing more about baseball than I did about the Bible.

I explained to her again that I was working for the Birmingham Black Barons and had to know what was going on with the team. She gave me one of her big humphs and went back to stirring the grits. She was making grits, eggs, and sausages, and those sausages were smelling good. I knew she'd be making redeye gravy, too, and she knew I was hungry.

Aunt Jack is my daddy's sister. They look a little bit alike, but Aunt Jack is darker than Daddy and Daddy's nose has a little more pinch to it than hers. Their father, Grandpap Owens, was an A.M.E. minister. Aunt Jack wants me to be a minister, or at least go to college. I was thinking about going to college when Daddy got hurt and couldn't work for almost five months. He's back at work now, but I am still working for the Black Barons. Maybe I'll go to college next year.

May 3

We split a doubleheader with Cleveland, and it was their first win of the season. Some of the Buckeyes were going on about how they liked Rickwood Field, and Bill Greason, our best pitcher, said that it was the best Negro League stadium in the whole country.

Most of the guys had played in major-league stadiums like the Polo Grounds up in New York, and Comiskey Park in Chicago. They said they were bigger than Rickwood Field but they weren't any better.

Pepper Bassett said they had to be better than Rickwood because they were built for white folks ball. Piper told him to keep his mind on his game and not to worry about white folks ball.

It's hard not to worry about white folks ball because now that Jackie Robinson is playing with the Brooklyn Dodgers and Larry Doby is playing with the Cleveland Indians, everybody is thinking about going up. Just a year ago, Jackie played with the Kansas City Monarchs, and Doby played with the Newark Eagles. Piper said that some of the players were so busy looking around for white scouts, they couldn't find the white ball.

Pepper is a huge dude. Wiley Griggs, who plays infield, said that Pepper is so big that when he was growing up his mama had to go out and buy some extra black just to keep him covered. He is too big to run fast and he can't hit all that good, but when he's in a good mood, which is once in a while, he's all right with me. When he isn't in a good mood, he isn't all right with anybody.

Piper gave me a copy of the opening day roster. I was sorry to see my name was not on it.

The 1948 Birmingham Black Barons

Lorenzo "Piper" Davis	*manager, second base*
John Britton	*third base*
Bill Greason	*pitcher*
Bill Powell	*pitcher*
Norman "Bobby" Robinson	*center field*
Joe Scott	*first base*
Ed Steele	*left field*
Sam Williams	*pitcher*
Arthur "Artie" Wilson	*shortstop*
Jim Zapp	*right field*
Jimmy Newberry	*pitcher*
Alonzo Perry	*pitcher, first base*
Herman Bell	*catcher*
Joe Bankhead	*pitcher*

Lloyd "Pepper" Bassett	• *catcher*
Jay Wilson	• *infield*
Wiley Griggs	• *infield*
Jehosie Heard	• *pitcher*
Clarence "Pijo" King	• *outfield*
William Morgan	• *pitcher*
Nat Pollard	• *pitcher*

May 4

One of the nice things about working for the Barons is that we get to travel all over the country. Pepper said that in two months every time somebody mentioned "home" we would all think of being on the bus. Our first trip was to Anniston, Alabama, where we played (and beat) the Buckeyes again. Sad Sam Jones, who lost the game, came over to the bus when we were loading up and started talking about how we were not that good a team when you broke it down man to man. I looked at Piper to see if he was going to say something back but he was just smiling from ear to ear.

On the way home we stopped at a small store to pick up some bread and cold cuts for supper. When me, Piper, Charlie Rudd, and Jimmy Zapp went into the store to get the stuff, the clerk acted as if he didn't see us, just kept on talking to a customer. They were both white, and so we figured we knew what that was about. When the clerk finally asked us what we wanted, Piper said that he needed food for twenty men. The clerk looked outside and saw the team bus and asked us were we the same Birmingham Black Barons that he had heard about.

Piper said we were. Then the clerk told us he could give us five loaves of bread and ten cans of sardines for twenty dollars. Piper said we were ballplayers, not fools, and there was no way they were going to pay that much for sardines and bread.

The clerk told Piper that he had better mind his manners, and Jimmy pulled Piper on out of the store before things got rough. When we got back on the bus, Pepper asked how come we didn't get the food and Piper told him what had happened. We didn't have anything to eat until we got back to Birmingham.

All of us were hungry and all of us were mad. Just about any white person could mess with you if you were black, and the thing was it made you mad for a little while and then it just left a hurt feeling inside of you.

When I got home my sister, Rachel, was sitting on a crate between Mama's legs, getting her hair braided. It was past seven, so I knew Daddy was off to the steel mill, where he worked. I looked in the icebox, and Rachel told me not to touch the potato salad because Aunt Jack had made it special for her. I told her to shut up because she was nothing but a half-pint, anyway. Then she said that was all right with her because men like little women.

Slap! Mama held Rachel by one of her braids and gave her a good slap. "You ain't old enough to smell your pee, girl!" Mama said. "Don't talk nothing in this house about what men like until you're grown! You hear me?"

There were some collard greens in the icebox, and I warmed them up with a ham hock and had that with some potato salad. It was good, too.

May 6

Pepper Bassett always wants to know what I'm writing in my notebook. I told him it's mostly about how the games are going and how the equipment is holding up. He told me not to write anything bad about him.

We're on the road again. Betsy, which is what Charlie Rudd calls the team bus, is running pretty good, and we are making good time. There are blankets and pillows on the overhead racks. The bats, bases, balls, and gloves are all kept in equipment bags in the luggage department. Once you get on the bus there are a thousand different smells. Bill Greason said that when the smell of fried chicken is stronger then the smell of the rubbing liniment it means the team is going good. All the players have their favorite spots. The veterans get the best seats.

We have two catchers, Pepper and Herman Bell. Bell said that the Monarchs are good, but no better than a half dozen other teams in the Negro Leagues. Only he was so tired, he was half asleep when he said it.

That's the thing, how tired everyone is. We played in Birmingham against the Buckeyes on Sunday, and as soon as the game was over we got on the bus and drove over to Anniston, where we played them again. Then we played against a team from the YMCA league, and finally a game against Bessemer Steel. Then we got right on our bus and were headed toward Cleveland.

May 8

My first time in Cleveland, Ohio, and it is a good city. They don't have all the WHITE and COLORED signs the way they have in Birmingham. Piper said that just because they didn't have signs all over the place didn't mean that we were welcome everywhere we went. It's just that when they didn't want Colored folks around they were more polite about it.

The big talk in Cleveland is Larry Doby. I asked Ed Steele, our left fielder, how good Doby is, and he said he was really good when he played with the Newark Eagles. He was also kind of quiet, like Jackie Robinson. It seems to me that what the major leagues are looking for are players who act in a certain way. That means you don't just have to be good but you have to act like the major-league teams want you to act. Piper said that when people yell things at Jackie from the stands, or when one of the players says something nasty to him about him being black, he doesn't answer them. That must be hard on him.

We played a single game in Cleveland, and then a doubleheader in Toledo.

There was an article in the Cleveland newspaper about whether the Red Cross should separate "white" blood from "Negro" blood. Pepper asked how they could tell once it came out of your body, and Bill said they could tell by the taste. Everybody gave him a look, but then he started laughing and we all laughed, except Pepper. He said he was thinking about breaking Bill's neck.

Jay Wilson is a skinny little guy with a high voice who always has something funny to say. He told Piper that he needed a rest because he's played so many ball games, he was dreaming about them. Bell asked him if he fielded as badly in his dreams as he did when he was awake.

That got Jay mad but not mad enough to mess with Bell, who has muscles in places some people don't even have places. Catchers are funny people.

Most of the guys don't mind traveling all over the country. Playing baseball pays more than most jobs, and it is a lot more fun. I think that if every Negro League team had a stadium of its own we could get more people to come to the games. When the Homestead Grays play in a big-league stadium, they draw at least as many fans as the white teams do. Another problem with our league is that our owners don't have the money to just pay us out of their pocket, so we have to get as many exhibition games as possible to keep the money coming in. That's why we travel so much.

Most of the complaining is good-natured. There isn't a man on the team who wants to give up baseball and do something else. Piper says that if any of his players is too tired to play ball, he should get into another line of work. He means it, too.

That was that. He doesn't care if we are tired or not. I don't get to play that much. I only get in games against the industrial league teams, and exhibition games, or the league games that we are really losing bad. Piper says if I can flatten out my swing I'll get into more games.

The exhibition games against other teams in the

Negro Leagues are hard, but games against colleges or strictly amateur teams are usually pretty easy. A lot of big companies have teams that play in what they call "industrial leagues." The Barons started off as an industrial team way back when.

May 9

The Barons played an exhibition game against the Homestead Grays. We won 4 to 3, but Buck Leonard hit a ball farther than I have seen any ball hit. Pepper said that you had to be a white man on a bus to go catch that ball, because if you were on the back of the bus where the Negroes sit, you never would catch up with it.

May 11

Lost to Cleveland in Montgomery. Me and Bill Greason went to the movies. No sooner had we settled in our seats in the Colored balcony than an usher came and said that all the Coloreds had to leave the theater. We asked why, and she said she didn't know, just that the manager told her it was so. A couple of people said they weren't going to leave, but a sheriff's deputy came up and told us all to go on downstairs right away or we would wish we had.

We got downstairs and we all had to line up against the wall while a white lady walked by us. Somebody had snatched a purse from her hand while she was walking, and she thought maybe he had run into the movie theater.

She looked us over and then said she didn't see the one who had snatched her purse.

I wanted to go back upstairs, but Bill was mad and said he was leaving the theater. They didn't give us our twenty cents back, either.

I did inventory tonight. We have eight gloves that belong to the team, nine bats, four bases, and the catcher's gear. Everything else belongs to the players. I think I'm going to buy my own glove.

May 14

I read in a magazine that Jackie Robinson had been a football star in college. He went to U.C.L.A., in California.

Piper asked me what the score had been for our first game of the season, and I looked it up in my journal and told him. That pleased him, and then everyone started telling me things to write down. Pepper and Ed Steele got into an argument over who was fastest: Cool Papa Bell or Sam Jethroe. Ed said he saw Sam Jethroe get a double on a bunt.

Pepper said that he had seen Cool Papa Bell walk into a hotel room, switch off the light, and get into bed before the room got dark. But then Artie Wilson said that one time Jesse Owens, who everybody said was the fastest man in the world, was on a field with Cool Papa Bell. He said that Cool Papa Bell had challenged Jesse to a race, and Jesse just smiled and said he had heard about Cool Papa. That settled it for most of us. Cool Papa Bell had to be the fastest if Jesse Owens did not want to run against him!

It took ten hours to reach Indianapolis yesterday. We got here at one o'clock in the morning. The hotel we stayed in was pretty beat-up looking, and we only got three rooms for the whole team. Pepper, Bill Powell, and Joe Bankhead slept on the bus.

May 15

The team we played today, the Indianapolis Clowns, came out and started fooling around, doing tricks with the ball and making people laugh. Piper said he didn't like that at all because it made it seem that Negro baseball teams weren't serious.

On one hand, everyone knows the major leagues are taking people like Jackie Robinson and Larry Doby because they aren't loud talking or clowning around. On the other hand, a team like the Clowns fools around before the ball game and sometimes even during the game if they can get away with it. The way I figure, they'll be the last ones to get into white folks ball.

Piper said when people see teams like the Clowns doing tricks with the ball or just being comical, they forget that they can play ball, too. I agree with Piper, but I really like to see the Clowns fooling around. They had this big guy on first base, Goose Tatum, and he was really funny. He could make the ball roll down his arm and then flex his muscle and make it pop up. When the game started he could hit, too. But we beat the Clowns, and I think everybody played harder against them because of what Piper had said. Sometimes Piper seems a little too tight, but when he says something, everybody listens to him. Everyone on our team was dead serious, and in the last inning, with us up by two runs, Pepper said something to their catcher, Sam Hairston. They got into pushing each other around, but there wasn't really a fight.

May 18

The Clowns came out today ready to play. They got a three-run lead and held it to the seventh inning. All their fans were screaming and carrying on. In the top of the eighth, Piper said he wanted to see what we were made of, and I knew he wanted to win bad.

Johnny Britton bunted the first pitch down the third baseline and beat it out. Everybody expected Herman to swing away, but he bunted, too, and got thrown out at first. When he came back to the dugout, Piper gave him a look that would have curdled milk. Wilson got up next and slapped a ball into right field for a double. That put men on second and third, and they walked Piper, which made him mad. He was even madder when the umpire called Ed Steele out on strikes.

The first pitch to Joe Scott was down in the dirt for a ball. The next one was high, but the ump called it a strike, anyway. The next pitch was a curve, and Scott must have missed it by a foot.

You could see the ball was dirtied up. Piper called time-out and asked to see the ball. The umpire told him to shut up and get back on base, and Piper said he had a right to see the ball. By this time a bunch of Clowns were standing around the mound and by the time they pro-duced the ball for Piper to see, it was a snow-white, brand-new ball. Piper complained to the umpire again and was told to get back on first base again. Soon as Piper got back on base, the pitcher started his pitching motion and Scott backed out of the batter's box.

I love to see Joe Scott when he gets mad, because the veins on the side of his head get swelled up and his eyes start bulging. He got back in the batter's box and hit the plate with the end of the bat.

Their pitcher, Bill Cathey, shook off one sign, then went into his full windup motion. He looked like he was going to throw fire up to the plate but when he came around, it was that same curveball again. Only this time the ball was white, and Scott lit into it. Man, he hit that ball a ton and a half! Their left fielder just stood out there and watched the ball go over his head. He didn't move because that ball was deep in the stands. Scott nodded his head up and down all the way around the bases. We were ahead 4 to 3.

When Piper got back into the dugout he said that anybody who made an error for the rest of the game was going to have to fight him right there on the field. The game ended with us winning 5 to 3.

May 20

Today we played a team in St. Louis called the Hops. They were an industrial league team and couldn't play at all the way I figured. Their pitcher was pretty wild and walked every other man he faced. When he slowed his ball down so he could get it over the plate, we were knocking it silly. I could have hit the guy easy. I know it. By the fifth inning we were ahead 12 to 0, and Piper told the guys to ease off. He didn't want to embarrass the team we were playing. If you embarrassed an amateur team, they wouldn't want to play you again.

Even when we eased off we were scoring runs. Pepper came in and hit a pop-up. The ball must have gone a mile high, and their second baseman missed it and Pepper started laughing. The final score was 18 to 2, but that wasn't the most exciting thing that happened. The stadium we played in had two dressing rooms, and we were changing clothes in one of them when these two white guys came in and stood by the door. One of them had a pistol stuck in his belt. I felt the hairs on the back of my neck stand up.

They asked us did we have a lot fun making their boys look bad. Piper said it was just a game and there was nothing to it.

The guy with the pistol told us to stick around if we wanted to play another game. He said he had some of his friends coming over and they played some pretty good baseball.

When the two guys left, everybody started grabbing their clothes. I asked Piper if we were going to play another game, and he told me to shut up and get the equipment on the bus.

I could tell by the way everybody was grabbing their stuff that Piper wasn't playing. We grabbed our stuff, put it in whatever bags we could find, and headed for the bus. Guys didn't even stop to change their clothes.

Charlie Rudd was sleeping on the bus when we got to it. Piper didn't even have to say anything to him. When Charlie saw us getting on in our uniforms, he started the bus up and, as soon as everybody was on, he moved it out.

I had seen that kind of thing before. Those guys weren't really mad about their team losing. They were just the kind of guys who knew that they could talk to black people any way they wanted to and wanted us to keep that in mind. Daddy said what they wanted us to remember was that we were supposed to stay "in our place."

May 21

The team gets paid twice a month for the regular games they play. When they play games like the one in St. Louis, which was just an exhibition game, they split the gate with the people who own the stadium and with the other team.

After the St. Louis game, Piper counted out the money and saw that the Barons' share was two hundred dollars. That came to eight dollars a man.

I only get a hundred dollars a month regular pay, but I get a full share of the split-up money and was pretty happy to get the eight dollars.

Afterward, Pepper, Alonzo Perry, Bell, Piper, and Sam Williams played Tonk, and Pepper lost his eight dollars. I'm glad I wasn't playing. I can't see working for money and then losing it in a card game. They play a lot of cards on the road. The games they play mostly are tonk, poker, and whist.

May 22, morning

Kansas City has a white owner, Mr. Wilkinson, and all the players like him a lot. He came to Street's, the hotel we were staying in, with a Colored reporter from the *Kansas City Call*. The reporter was asking him and Buck O'Neil what they thought would be the future of the Negro Leagues if the major leagues kept taking players. Mr. Wilkinson, who's pretty old and wears thick glasses, said the Negro Leagues would last as long as the south lasted.

The reporter from the *Call*, whose name was Davis, asked Mr. Wilkinson if he thought the south would last. Mr. Wilkinson looked at him and asked him to repeat the question, and he did. Then Mr. Wilkinson said that the south would last a lot longer than some people thought it would. Buck O'Neil said that the Negro Leagues could be just like the minor leagues and could even get support from the major leagues.

Afterward everyone was talking about how nice Mr. Wilkinson was and how he was one of the first people to have night baseball. But I was thinking of the reporter from the *Kansas City Call*. I asked him how he got his job, and he said he had gone to college and worked on the college magazine. He asked me if I wanted to be a reporter, and I told him I was thinking about it.

May 22, evening

Piper told me to write down why we had lost, only he didn't say *lost* — he said we had our butts kicked. He said he was going to send what I wrote down off to the *Birmingham World* and see that they publish it.

We were sitting in the dugout between games and Piper was mad. Piper was a man who could get mad in a heartbeat. Before the game he was talking about how we had to establish something against the Kansas City Monarchs. What happened was that Kansas City established something against us.

We went down one two three in the first inning. Jim LaMarque, their pitcher, was throwing hard and throwing strikes. In the bottom of the first, with Bankhead pitching, their first two batters walked. That was Curt Roberts and Herb Souell. Bankhead got Gene Baker to pop up, but then Elston Howard hit a line drive into the stands, and they were ahead 3 to 0. Piper called a meeting at the pitcher's mound and told everybody to tighten up their defense. The next batter, Hank Thompson, got a triple and Willard Brown got a single and we were down by four runs. Piper took Bankhead out and brought in Jehosie Heard and Buck O'Neil got a double off his first pitch.

Kansas City was just good. Okay, that was one thing. But when Piper came into the dugout after the fifth inning (we were losing by eight runs then) and Bankhead was looking at a newspaper clipping, things got ugly.

He yelled at Bankhead because he was reading in the dugout instead of paying attention to the game. Somebody had given Bankhead a newspaper clipping about Jackie Robinson stealing home against Pittsburgh.

Piper blew up. He got the clipping from Bankhead and threw it on the floor of the dugout. We lost the game big time.

Jimmy Newberry pitched the second game and we won. Britton hit a ground ball to Souell with two outs in the ninth and the Monarch's third baseman let it go through his legs. Two runs scored and we won 4 to 3.

Nobody said anything when we got on the team bus and went back to the hotel. We were playing in Kansas City, Missouri, but the hotel was across the river in Kansas City, Kansas. We ate at the Blue Sky Diner down the street from the hotel and the food wasn't that good. They served white gravy with their chops, and it was greasy. Bill Greason said the only thing they could make in Kansas City was steak and barbecue and I believe him. Piper finished eating first, paid, and left. Then the team relaxed some.

Some of the guys went downtown to a jazz club. I wanted to go, too, but Piper keeps an eye on me and he had told me to stick with Bill Greason. I told Bill we should go to see if we could hear some good, fast jazz and check out the ladies. Instead we went back to the hotel.

There was a phone in the lobby, and I called home. I don't know why I did and I really didn't have anything to say. Rachel answered, and I told her to put Mama on. She asked me where I was and I told her in Kansas City and she started asking me what Kansas City looked like. I told her to shut up and put Mama on. She said for me to beg her.

Right then and there I decided not to ever get married. I couldn't imagine myself married to no woman like Rachel. When she did get Mama on the phone, I just asked her how everything was going and she asked me what Kansas City was like, the same as Rachel.

I was glad to talk to Mama. After I hung up I thought of something else to say and almost called back. Traveling was nice. Home was good, too.

May 24

Lost two games against the Chicago American Giants yesterday. Greason said that it would be wise for us to keep a clear distance away from Piper, who does not like to lose. We lost the first game 7 to 5 and the second game 5 to 3. I think everybody is just tired. Piper was yelling for everybody to run out their ground balls. Jimmy Zapp struck out and ran to first base, and everybody had to smile at that, even Piper.

Tonight we played a night game against the Monarchs in Louisville, Kentucky. The field was small and kind of dark, but the Monarchs had their own night lights, which they could move from ballpark to ballpark. Very nice.

We won the game 5 to 4. Instead of being glad, Piper just said that we should have won all our games against the Monarchs. But I think he's wrong, because the Monarchs are one good team.

"Pijo," which is what they call Clarence King, said that his brother's dog had had puppies and asked if anybody wanted one. I said yes and hope that Mom is going to let me bring it home.

The newspaper is going on about how Truman is going to integrate the army. Bell said it didn't mean anything, because the war was already over, but Perry said it meant a lot, and he explained that the two biggest things they had in the United States were the armed forces and major-league baseball. They had baseball integrated and if they integrated the army it was going to mean that Negroes were going to be equal for the first time.

I couldn't help wondering what that meant. A lot of people were saying that the Negro Leagues were going to fold up because people wanted to see integrated baseball. I wondered if integration in everything would mean there would be nothing Negro anymore.

We had to travel to Memphis, Tennessee, and after packing up the equipment I went with Charlie to get the bus gassed up. Then we picked up the team and started. We had bought some barbecue ribs from a Colored restaurant, and just out of town we stopped for some pop and coffee from a white diner. We had to go around to the back to get them. The ribs were good, and we ate them on the bus.

May 25

It took us two hours short of forever to get to Tennessee. A lot of the problems getting there were because of Jimmy Zapp, who had to keep stopping and finding a place to go to the bathroom. He said he must have eaten something bad, but Bill Powell said that the Zapper had eaten so many barbecued ribs that if he had saved the bones he could have built a small house for himself.

It was morning when we finally arrived, and we took a vote if we wanted to get hotel rooms or sleep on the bus to save money. Everybody voted to go to sleep on the bus, and Charlie parked in a Colored park. A state trooper at the park asked us who we were, and Charlie told him we were the Birmingham Black Barons, the best baseball team in the south. The trooper said he had gone to a few Negro games about three years before, when Josh Gibson was playing. He asked Charlie if we played with a regular baseball, and Charlie said sure we do. Perry threw the trooper a ball. The state trooper looked it over and shook his head. He said he still didn't see how in the world Gibson could hit a ball as far as he did.

Perry asked the trooper if he had ever heard of Babe Ruth and, when the trooper said he had, Perry told him that Ruth was the white Josh Gibson, only a little smaller.

The state trooper gave Perry the ball back and said he had never seen anybody hit the ball like Gibson, and he was sure surprised that Negroes had the same kind of ball that whites had.

We parked the bus and got a few more hours sleep. We changed into our uniforms right there on the bus before heading toward the stadium.

On the way over to the stadium I wondered how that trooper could think that we used a different kind of ball. I said that to Piper, and Piper said that a lot of white people just don't know what being a Negro is all about. That did not make a whole lot of sense to me.

May 26

When we arrived at the ball field all the guys were dead tired, but once they walked out onto the field it was as if they got new life in them. The Chicago American Giants were a good team, but not all that good. Piper, as usual, was talking about how the team needed to bear down. He said that on paper we were the better team, but the game was not being played on paper and we had better show some hustle on the field.

The crowd was enthusiastic, but the park wasn't nearly as nice as Rickwood. It seemed a little better when we won, 5 to 1.

After the game most of the guys stayed at the hotel that Piper booked for us, but a few were staying with Negro families around town. Bill Greason wanted to see a cousin he knew and asked if I wanted to go, and I said no. That's how I got to go to a pool hall with Herman Bell, Pepper, and Jehosie Heard.

In the pool hall there was this tall guy who looked like he needed to be arrested for something! He wore a powder-blue zoot suit with wide shoulders, a blue snap-brim hat, and a white silk shirt that was open down the front. On his side he wore this gold chain that went from the front of his pants down the leg and into the pocket. He had a scar down one side of his face that started just in front of his ear, went down the side of his jaw, and disappeared under his ear. Bell said that he was a pool hustler and his name was Mambo. Anyway, this Mambo guy had a girl with him. She was wearing a little short tight dress and she started winking and making up to us as soon as she found out we were ballplayers. This Mambo guy pulled back his coat, and you could see he had a pistol in his belt. He said he thought it was time for us to go.

I thought Pepper and Bell would have been all over him, but they just said they thought it was time to go.

It was hot in Chicago, and the poolroom had been even hotter. There was a little breeze outside. I asked Pepper what that had been about. Pepper said a lot of girls flirt with ballplayers and they don't mind a bit if they cause a little trouble.

May 27

I am so tired, I can't see straight. My pencil broke, and I asked Jay Wilson could I borrow his and he told me no and to leave him alone. Jay's not like that, but he's tired, too. I'm missing home again but I am determined not to call every time I get a little lonely.

Beat the Giants again. Quincy Trouppe is their manager and he catches for them. Piper said he was better than Campanella when he was younger. I never saw Campanella play, so I don't know. I told that to Piper, and he told me to shut up, too.

The bus broke down, and we are going to take a train to Atlanta.

May 28

This afternoon in Atlanta we played against a team called the Black Crackers. They were a good team, a lot better than we thought they would be, and we really had to play some good ball to come from behind and beat them. After the game we were tired, but the players were feeling good and a little loosey-goosey. Even Piper was relaxed. We got down to the train station, and he was talking to everybody about how we were looking like a real ball club.

It was raining lightly, and we were in a good mood at the station. Then the train that would have taken us to Birmingham came in, but the conductor said we couldn't get on it because they had taken the Colored car off for repair. What we saw on the train was a big group of white men who were going to a convention in Birmingham. The train was crowded, and they didn't want us on. The next train wasn't going to be leaving until nearly two o'clock in the morning.

As good as we had been feeling, we came down in a big hurry. The Barons shuffled back into the station and into the Colored waiting room. We all just sat there for a while, with some of the players getting real mad at what had happened and others just stretching out on the benches. Then a fat, brown-skinned fellow came and asked us if were the Black Barons from Birmingham who couldn't get on the train, and we said yes. He said he was from the First Baptist Church and his congregation would love for us to spend the night at their church. He had a bus, and so we went to his church and had a good time. They fed us and treated us really nice.

I wanted to say something to Piper that maybe just winning ball games did not mean all that much at times, but I don't think he would have understood. I think what he would have said was that when you played ball you could win or lose depending on how good you were and how the ball bounced. Being black did not make a difference.

May 29

Home and Rickwood Field never looked so good. When I got home I gave Mama a big kiss, and she told me not to get upset with my room. I didn't know what that was supposed to mean, but when I got to it the whole place stunk like cocoa butter. Mama had let some of Rachel's friends stay over, and two girls had slept in my room and left some of their hair stuff on my dresser. I told Rachel she should keep her friends out of my room, and she said it wasn't my room anymore, that Mama just lets me stay there when I come to visit. I got mad and wanted to say something to her but I couldn't think of anything to say. I felt too bad about what she had said.

We were playing the Clowns again. This guy named Andy Mesa was on first, and Tatum, their first baseman, hit a single just past Piper. Okay, so Mesa goes tearing around second base and bearing down on third, and everybody starts yelling because they know he's going to try to score all the way from first on that little dinky single. Bobby Robinson comes in and scoops the ball up and fires it in to Bassett, who's catching. Mesa is round third and coming down the line. Bassett, he's got the line covered, the plate covered, and he's waiting with the ball when Mesa plows into him.

The umpire called Mesa out, and we went over to Bassett, who was lying on the ground, to see if he was all right. He was lying there grinning and holding the ball, and we all went back to the dugout. But when Bassett came back to the dugout, he was rubbing his arm. When Piper asked him if he wanted to come out, he didn't say anything, just grumbled under his breath the way he does sometime. Piper told Bell to put the catcher's gear on.

I saw Bassett's arm. It was scraped up something terrible and bled right through his uniform.

Charlie Richards, who is white and is the clubhouse boy for the white Barons, got a bandage for Bassett and helped put it on. Charlie comes to a lot of the Black Barons' games because he likes good baseball.

I asked Mom if it would be all right to take a dog from Pijo, and Daddy said yes even before she answered. I went over to Pijo's house and got the puppy. Pijo's sister is a little, kind of nervous, woman with a nice voice. She told me to take good care of the dog, which I would have done, anyway. On the way home he peed on me. I was going to name him "River" but I decided to name him "Skeeter" instead. No special reason except that I just like the name.

May 30

Played a doubleheader against the Memphis Red Sox here in Little Rock. We played well and split the games. The whole team was invited to a church picnic, but we have to play the Red Sox again in a few days back in Birmingham so we left as soon as the second game was over.

On the bus we played whist and me and Piper played the first game against Jimmy Newberry and Alonzo Perry. We were playing rise and fly style, meaning that whoever lost had to get up and let somebody else play against the winners. Guess who got mad at me when we lost???? Piper said he knew a blind monkey who could play cards better than me, and I did not think that was a good thing to say.

Life on the road can be boring. I like seeing all the cities but bouncing along in the bus or sleeping on some hard bed in a cheap hotel is not my idea of paradise. If I go to college I would have more things I could do. On the other hand if I played good enough to get into the major leagues I could play there for a while and then go to college. I told that to Bill Greason, and he said he could just imagine my face on a baseball card. Piper said I should stick with baseball cards because I sure couldn't play regular cards. He didn't have to say that.

June 1

In rained, so I spent the day cleaning up all the equipment. It all looks good, and Piper said I was a good equipment manager. I asked him if he thought I would get into a game soon, and he said yes. Aunt Jack tried to get Daddy and Mommy to go to a concert given by the Wings Over Jordan Choir. They had just come back from entertaining soldiers in Europe, and everybody was saying how good they were. Nobody went with Aunt Jack, and she made a speech about we were old-time Negroes and it was time for a new Negro in America.

Joe Bankhead called me and said that Piper had cut him from the team. He was mad. Then he cried.

I had a talk with Rachel. I told her it was okay for her to let her friends use my room while I am on the road but not to let them go into my stuff. She said she might sleep in my bed. The girl is pushing me.

June 2

Ed Steele said I would not believe New Orleans, and he was right. It is the biggest city in the world. We got in and went to a hotel called Pascals, or something like that. All day long we walked along Canal Street and then went over to what they call the French Quarter. Bill Greason said a man could lose his soul in New Orleans and not even notice it. I said uh-huh, but I don't know what he meant by that.

June 3

We are playing the Memphis Red Sox, and they are traveling with us. Their regular bus broke down, and they're traveling in three cars that break down every five miles. Some of them wanted to ride in our bus, and Piper said no. It has to be hard riding seven guys to a car, which is what they are doing, but one of their guys said it wasn't so bad. He said he was making more money than anybody he knew. All the time he was talking he was also chewing on a big cigar and showing off a flashy ring that he wore on his pinkie. When the Memphis player left, Pepper said that his cigar was probably smarter than he was.

June 4

We have won two games against Memphis and lost one
because of a bad call. In the game we lost the score was 6
to 5 in our favor, and we only needed one more out in the
ninth. The Memphis left fielder tried to score from third
on a short fly ball, and Jim Zapp threw a perfect ball to
Bell. The guy was out by about a mile and a half, but the
umpire called him safe. I couldn't believe it.

June 5

Lots of excitement this week. Word got around that there
was going to be a protest demonstration in downtown
Birmingham. They are going to protest against Carroll's
Restaurant, which doesn't serve Coloreds anymore.

Carroll's did not really ever let Negroes eat in their
restaurant. They had their tables and they had a counter
the cash register sat on. If you were a Negro you could
give them an order for food to take out, then sit on one of
the chairs along the wall until they brought it out in a
sack. When they fixed the place up they took away the
counter, and now they said they didn't have takeout food,
either.

Elder Williams, from Sixteenth Street Baptist, wants
to have an outdoor meeting over in Gadsden Park, but I

heard Daddy saying that a lot of people are kind of nervous about it. President Truman is doing a lot for Negroes, and people do not want to make trouble.

I am all for having a protest demonstration. As far as I am concerned there isn't any reason for anybody not to serve Colored. And yet just about anywhere you go you see the COLORED and WHITE signs telling you where you can go and can't go.

I got to the park early for the game against the Monarchs. The dirt at Rickwood is really good, and some men from the Boston Red Sox were there packing some of it in boxes. They were going to take it to Boston to rub the balls with during the game. The white Barons are the farm team of the Boston Red Sox.

We played the Monarchs, and Ed Steele hit a low line drive that hit second base and bounced straight up in the air. The Monarchs' second baseman got the ball and tried to get Ed out when he rounded first base. He hit Ed with the ball, and when Ed took off and ran to second, their first baseman threw the ball and hit him again. It was an accident, but that didn't stop Ed from getting mad.

June 7

Sunday we won a doubleheader against the Monarchs. The first game was 4 to 3 and the second 5 to 4.

Today we played a day game against Howard University and creamed them with Yours Truly playing right field for three innings. I caught one fly ball and got a single. Piper said I looked good up at bat. On the bench the guys were talking about whether we were Negroes, Colored, or Afro-Americans. Pepper said they could call him anything they wanted to as long as they did not call him late for dinner.

Then we played a night game against the Monarchs (with me on the bench) and won 7 to 3.

June 8

Rachel is going to take piano lessons from Mr. Parrish. She was taking lessons from Sister Purvis, but the only thing Sister Purvis knew was church music, and Mama asked Daddy if he would pay for lessons from Mr. Parrish and he said okay.

Rachel said she wanted to learn how to play jazz music. When Aunt Jack heard her say that, I thought she was going to have a two-toned fit.

"Just ignore her," Mama said. "We ordered her some sense from Sears Roebuck, but it ain't got here yet."

Oh, yes. I asked Daddy about the question of being Colored, or Negro, or Afro-American. He said he was so busy running from *nigger* that he hadn't had a chance to grab anything else.

June 10

The bus broke down again. Mr. Hayes got some friends of his to drive the team up to East St. Louis, Illinois, where we played in a dinky little park. Ed Steele got hit by a pitch again, and Pepper said that he must have a magnet in his head that attracted baseballs, and Ed said some things to Pepper that I will not put down in this journal.

Charlie met us with the bus in Centralia. When we were on the bus Jimmy Newberry and Joe Scott started talking about the protest against Carroll's again, with Jimmy saying that the Black Barons should lead it.

Jimmy Zapp said he thought that people's hearts were changing and that segregation couldn't last forever.

"Yes, it can," Joe said. "During the war they had some black soldiers from the Ninety-second guarding German prisoners over in Kentucky. The prisoners were out cleaning the roads. You know they had to take the prisoners into diners to eat and they let the Germans in to eat but the Colored soldiers had to eat outside. Now, if they let the enemy eat in the diners and kept our boys out, you know they mean to keep it that way."

June 14

When we got home Mama had a sty on her eye. Aunt Jack put a potato in some cheesecloth and put it on the sty.

I told Daddy what Joe had said. He listened to me real careful and then he said there were so many things wrong with the world and that there weren't a lot of good answers to all the questions I had in me. He said he was sorry, as if he personally had done something wrong.

June 16

The Birmingham Black Barons are the best team in the league. We are drawing good crowds at Rickwood and every place else.

I heard Mr. Hayes say that the Newark Eagles were having trouble big time. The Eagles don't have their own field, and they also face competition from the New York Yankees, the New York Giants, and the Brooklyn Dodgers, as well as the New York Black Yankees, and Cuban Giants. That was just too much competition.

We played an exhibition game against the Alliance Stars up in Columbus and won easily, 9 to 2. I pinch-hit for Perry, who was pitching, and got a walk. Also, Wiley Griggs, who talks so bad all the time, got into a fight and he swings like a girl!

June 17

Indianapolis again. When we were driving in there was a big sign on the side of the road. It said, WELKOME TO KLAN KOUNTRY. The three Ks were larger than the other letters and colored red. Pepper said that the Ku Klux Klan wanted everybody to know that they were around in Indianapolis. Bill Greason said it was a miracle that an organization that did so many evil things talked so much about being Christians.

We played a four-team doubleheader. Indianapolis played against the Monarchs in the first game, and we played against the Newark Eagles in the second game. Newark looked good, and Piper wanted us to look good, so he pitched Bill Powell. They had a guy named Monte Irvin, who they said was a cinch to go up to the major leagues. I had a chance to talk to him, and he was a nice guy. He had a way of smiling at you that made you smile back. I watched him in the field and he was all right, nothing special, and I was anxious to see him bat.

Piper told Powell that the only thing Irvin couldn't hit was a low inside pitch. Powell's first pitch was low and inside and fast. Irvin hit it against the left field wall so hard, it bounced halfway back to the infield and Irvin ended up on second. Powell looked over at Piper, and Piper just shrugged.

Jimmy Wilkes was the next batter, and Powell pitched him a slow curve. Wilkes hit the ball so far out of the park, I thought it might go all the way to Birmingham. We lost the game 6 to 0, and Piper was mad again. That man really hates to lose.

June 20

Back in Birmingham. Our baseball season is divided into two halves. Whoever wins the first half plays the winner of the second half to see who wins the pennant. Then the winner of the pennant in the Negro National League plays the winner of the Negro American League in the Negro League World Series. It looks like the Barons are going to win the first half, and I think we're going to win both halves! Yes!

I got home, and Mama and Aunt Jack made roast turkey with oyster stuffing, deviled eggs, candied yams, spinach, and macaroni for Father's Day. Daddy sat at one end of the table, and I got to sit at the other end because we were the men in the house. This put Rachel's nose out of joint, which was good.

Mama had cut out an article from the white newspaper about the planned protest over at Carroll's. Aunt Jack said that somebody must have blabbed about the protest and that black people had to learn to keep their mouths shut.

I read the article Mama had cut out and saw that a Mr. Eugene Connor, who used to announce some of the games at Rickwood for the white Barons, said that if the Negroes had a protest downtown, white people should arm themselves in case of trouble.

I also bought ten pairs of wool socks from Charlie Richards for one dollar and forty cents and sold four pairs to Pepper, three to Alonzo Perry, and one to Joe Scott for twenty cents apiece. That's already a profit of twenty cents and I still have two pairs left. Charlie also gets fifty cents per player from the white Barons for running the same errands I do for free. I will have to talk some more to Charlie about his side business.

June 22

Had some trouble at Hornet Stadium in Montgomery. We were playing against Alabama State University. Some white guys who were watching the game and drinking got stupid and were making remarks on the sidelines. They were saying that the National League was looking for a black ball to play with now that so many Coloreds were getting into the major leagues. All their dumb talk didn't bother the Barons so much as it did the college kids. They wanted to play well but they kept paying attention to the guys on the side and making errors.

Piper said that's what they wanted, to get the players thinking about them and not the game.

Piper put me in the game in the sixth inning and told me not to pay any attention to the guys on the side. I got up to bat and kept telling myself that I wasn't going to pay them any mind. I was so busy thinking about how I wasn't going to be thinking about them that I didn't get near the ball. I really felt bad when I walked away from the plate. They had half my mind on hitting and the other half on dealing with them.

The guys doing all the talking were standing down the third baseline. When Ed Steele got up he said something to the catcher, who ran out to the pitcher. The next pitch was slow and inside. Ed lined that ball right past the head of the guys making all the nasty remarks. You should have seen them scramble!

June 23

I was lying in bed thinking, and Rachel came into the room and asked me if she could borrow a dollar. I said she could take one off the dresser. She took the dollar and then she asked me what I was thinking, and I told her what had happened yesterday with the white guys at the park making remarks and how I had struck out. She said it was because I was a chump and could not hit, anyway.

She told me she could hit if she had a chance. I told her it wasn't true that I was a chump, but it was true that I was a Negro and had to think about it all the time. I had to think about it when I got on a bus, when I took a drink from a water fountain, when I walked into a store. I told Rachel it was a wonder that Negroes managed to do anything when they had to think about race all the time.

She said I was trying to be a deep thinker but I was not making it. I asked her how it felt to be as old as she was and still be looking like an ironing board, flat on top and skinny on the bottom.

June 24, morning

It rained all last night, and the field at Talladega College was soggy. We were playing in Talladega, Alabama, and there were about a million girls at the game, mostly from the college. I was standing on the side and one girl, she was tall, and her skin was just the color of a ripe peach, kept looking at me. She had a nice, round face on her, and pretty eyes. She gave me a big lots-of-teeth smile, and I gave her one right back. She asked me what I was doing after the game. I told her I had to check with the manager.

I asked Piper if it was all right if I stayed over in Talladega for a few hours, and he told me to get my butt on the bus.

I went back and told the girl they needed me to make arrangements in the next city and I had to leave right after the game, but I got her address. Her name is Jasmine Hinton, and I am pretty sure I am deeply in love with her. Also, she is seventeen.

June 25

Mama's eye is still infected, and Daddy said she needs to go to the hospital or to see Dr. Epps. I know that made Aunt Jack mad because she thinks she can heal anything. One time she made me wear a clove of garlic around my neck for a whole month so I wouldn't catch a cold. That garlic was okay if you didn't sweat but if you started sweating, it would start in to stinking.

Joe Bankhead came around to Rickwood. He was still mad because Piper let him go. He said he wasn't given a real chance and then he said he hoped we lost the rest of our games. Piper said he had an attitude problem, and I agree.

I think I will shoot, skin, and then stuff Rachel. The first thing I did was swear her to secrecy, and she raised her right hand and said she swore. Then I told her about Jasmine. I wasn't bragging on it or anything like that but I had called Jasmine and she had told me she thought I was good-looking. She added it was not just because I was a ballplayer, too.

Back to Rachel. I had to go with Mama to the beauty parlor because of her bad eye. She wanted to get her hair done at Ann's Beauty Shop over on Seventeenth Street before she went to the doctor.

She said she looked terrible with her eye all swoll up and did not want to scare Dr. Epps into a heart attack. I said she did not look that bad, but she did.

Rachel was going, too, and I knew she wanted to have her hair done but Mama said she just needed to get her kitchen straightened and she could do that at home with a hot comb. When we got to the beauty parlor Pearl Grant was there, and so was Lucille Davis, Elder Davis's daughter, who made dresses. They're all churchgoing ladies but as soon as they got together they started talking about who was sneaking around with who.

Miss Davis said that she heard that Drusilla, Ernestine's sister, was sitting up on a bar stool down at the Savoy for so long, her leg went numb and she fell off. Then she said that Drusilla went to church over at Metropolitan and if she spent as much time praying as she did backsliding, her knees would be as shiny as the dirty clothes she wore.

Then Rachel just had to open her big mouth and ask if my new girlfriend looked anything like Drusilla.

Mama gave me a look, and I made-believe I was reading a magazine as Rachel blabbed her big mouth.

Dr. Epps said that Mama's sty was going away and gave her something to wash her eye out with and told her to be careful it didn't spread to the other eye. Then, all the way home, I had to hear how Mama would rather go stone-blind than see me running around with a loose woman.

When we got home Daddy was home, and Mama told him that I had a girlfriend on the road and that he knew what kinds of girls were on the road. Daddy said he understood. Mama said she was so hurt, she had to go and lie down. Rachel said it was a shame that I hurt the woman who brought me into the world.

I told Daddy that Jasmine is not a road girl but a college girl. He told me not to talk about it anymore. "Just put it in the corner and let it lie there until it dies," he said.

June 27

Everybody's upset. We played the Red Sox in Memphis, and the crowd was so small, the Memphis owner wanted to cancel the game. They decided to let people in off the street at half price, and then some of the people in the stands got mad because they had paid a full dollar to get in.

The Memphis Red Sox have this guy named Willie

Wells, Jr. who everybody talks about. They call him "the Devil," and sure enough it was he who beat us.

We had the bases loaded in the top of the ninth with two outs and Joe Scott up with three balls and no strikes. All we needed was one more ball to walk in a run. And if Jones, who they called Casey, pitched to Scott, I knew Scott was going to tear the ball up. Okay, so Britton is on third base, and Wells, the Red Sox third baseman, is talking to him a mile a minute and when he's not talking to him, he's yelling at the pitcher. Britton is laughing, and Wells runs out to the pitcher and tells him to calm down.

Then Wells came back to third base and said something to Britton, which made him laugh even more. Then Britton stepped off the base, Wells tagged him out with the ball he had hidden in his glove, and the game was over Guess who was mad after the game?

June 28

On the way to Atlanta, Pepper was driving the bus to give Charlie Rudd a rest. Pepper went through a red light, and a highway patrolman pulled us over. The patrolman asked Pepper if had seen the red light. Pepper said he had seen it but since he was from up north he was not sure what it meant. He said he thought maybe green lights were for white folks and black folks had to go with the red light.

The patrolman stuck his thumbs in his belt, then figured out Pepper was making a joke, and started laughing. Then he told Pepper to get moving.

Atlanta is a pretty city and about as busy a place as you can get. We parked the bus, and some of us just walked around and looked at what there was to see. Piper asked me to pick up some film for him, and that was why I walked into the five-and-dime. I wasn't even thinking about anything except for Piper telling me to pick up some film for his camera. He said there were two kinds of film, number 120 and number 620, and for me to get the 620 film.

That was what was on my mind. I went in and asked if they had any film number 620. The clerk said to wait and she would go ask the manager. I sat down at the counter and was thinking about that film when a woman behind the counter asked me what I wanted. I looked up and saw that she had a bottle of pop in her hand, so I asked her for a bottle of pop and a doughnut.

"We don't serve no nigras here," she said. "Get on up off that seat."

She was a big woman with stringy white hair and a tooth missing. When I looked around, two white kids sitting at the counter were looking at me and I felt really ashamed. I got up and stood off from the counter. The white woman behind the counter came around and wiped off the seat where I had been sitting. She looked at me like I was dirt or something before she went back around the counter.

I looked at the white kids, and they were still looking at me. I think they felt as bad for me as I did for me. Also, *nigra* was a name I had forgot about.

Fourth of July

Rickwood Field. I don't ever get completely rested anymore. Soon as we play in one city it's pile on the bus and get to the next one.

Pepper hurt his finger blocking the plate against the Clowns. He's got big fat fingers to begin with, and when one of them is swollen it's about as big as my wrist.

The big thing was that Aunt Jack, Mama, and Daddy came to the ball game. I told Piper my family was there and asked if I could get into the game. Aunt Jack almost never came to a game, and Daddy said that she wasn't going to enjoy herself no matter what. I knew that was right because as far as I could tell, church women, especially the saved ones, did not like to show themselves having too much fun.

Piper gave the team a big lecture about how we needed to play hard and give the folks a good show because the league was in trouble. He was saying that people wanted to follow the Colored players in the major leagues. He said if we weren't going to play good ball we might as well fold up the league. Some teams were having a hard time even meeting the payroll.

That was all right for Piper to say, but the guys sitting on the bench were mostly thinking about playing in the major leagues, too. I could not help but go through the *Birmingham World* and look for stories on Jackie Robinson, Larry Doby, Roy Campanella, and Satchel Paige. It was just a natural thing to do.

I had seen most of them play and, except for Satchel Paige, they just about fit into the same category as the rest of the players in the Negro Leagues. Then I started thinking that maybe I would play on a team in the major leagues. If I did I thought I would most like to play on the New York Yankees. I could play right field if DiMaggio was playing center. That would work.

Mays, the new guy, was playing in Bobby Robinson's place in the outfield because Bobby had hurt his leg sliding. It was a break but not a bad break, and we expected him back soon.

We played a doubleheader and won the first and lost the second game. After the games Mama asked me if I wanted to go on a picnic with the church, and I told her the team was going to Memphis that night. She told Daddy maybe I shouldn't go. Daddy didn't answer, and I knew he was letting it lie till it died.

Mama said that playing baseball wasn't a real job and that I was still her son and she still had some say-so when it came to her flesh and blood. Daddy said it paid real money and so it was a real job and that was that.

The truth was that playing baseball did pay good. Not many jobs paid three hundred dollars a month, which is what most of the Barons make, and that didn't even take in the extra games where we just made whatever we could and split it up between us. My grandfather on my Mama's side, Booker T. Smith, told me he never made more than forty dollars a week in his life. I know Daddy makes seventy-four dollars a week, not counting overtime. Sometimes with overtime he makes close to ninety dollars.

Aunt Jack gave me a bag with fried chicken with pepper and lemon sauce wrapped up in a waxed paper, and also a jar of potato salad. A lot of the guys had food in bags, and when we got on the bus it was smelling like a picnic. I tried to wait until we got to Memphis to eat, but when everybody else started eating, I did, too. That chicken was some good.

It took four and a half hours to reach Memphis, and everybody was tired. When we got to the motel we were supposed to be staying in, the owner said he didn't have any more room because a church group had come in. Piper said if he didn't find us some room he was going to let the ballplayers tear his motel apart. The owner, a little fat man with thick glasses and a shiny suit, told us to go down the road and tear up the white man's motel.

Piper calmed down and asked the guy in the shiny suit about some other places that rented to Coloreds, and he told us of a place. We got back in the bus, and Charlie drove us over to the new place. It was in a quiet neighborhood, and the owner said she was glad to have the business. We found out that she owned a bar, a restaurant, and an undertaker parlor. Since nobody was being buried, we could use the parlor.

July 5

It is now official. We have won the first half of the season and we got a telegram from the *Birmingham World* congratulating us. It's going to be announced in the next paper. Willie Morgan, who hardly ever said anything, brought a sign and put it up in the dugout.

RULES FOR ALL GUESTS

1. KEEP THIS HOUSE RESPECTABLE.
2. NO LOUD TALKING.
3. NO DRINKING.
4. NO GAMBLING.
5. NO SHOWING YOUR COLOR.

It was one of those signs you see on some Colored motels, and Pijo and Will Morgan got into a fight when Pijo said some black people were not going to be happy with integration because it was just going to make it hard on them. Will said that only ignorant fools like Pijo would have a hard time, and Pijo smacked him. Then Pepper jumped into it to separate them and hurt his finger again. Piper said he was going to fine everybody, and Pijo said he didn't care because he didn't have any money, anyway.

Will Morgan had thought the sign was funny, but I did not think it was funny at all. If black people did not think much of themselves, I don't know how we should expect white people to think we are as good as they are. I do not think I should be ashamed to show my color.

We played against the Clowns and beat them easy. I don't think the Clowns were trying too hard.

After the second game in Memphis we got on the bus again and rode 110 miles to Greenwood, Mississippi, to play a night game. The Clowns, who we were playing in Greenwood, borrowed an old bus from the city to get there. It was a pretty good bus with plenty of room. When they were getting on the bus Piper made some remarks that they weren't much of a ball team and he wondered if they minded getting beat three times in one day.

I told Bill Greason that I thought Piper was getting touchy. Bill said the times were touchy. He said that if the white folks took all the best players from our league, we could fold up. The interesting part of it for me was that for years people were saying that white folks only wanted to see white ballplayers. But nobody ever said that black folks only wanted to see black ballplayers. I thought about it on the bus and figured out that what was happening was that we were trying to prove to white people that we could do things as well as they could. I thought that was pretty good and said it to Bill Greason, who has more sense than most people. Bill asked me how the black ballplayers in the majors were doing. I said they were doing great, and he said he guessed the white folks must have known all along what they could do, and where to find them.

It took three hours to get to Greenwood, and Piper said we weren't going to stay. So we played the Clowns again, beat them again with Bill Greason pitching, and then drove all the way back to Birmingham. The bus went off the road once when Charlie fell asleep. Lucky for us he just went up a little embankment, and nobody was hurt. Jimmy Zapp said not to wake him up for an almost-accident. "Just shake me if I get killed," he said.

Playing so many games in a row is rough, but every time we play we make money and that's what it's all about. Most of the guys on the team have families and it helps a lot to make a few extra dollars. Bill Greason said that one day he would be able to tell his children about how hard he worked for them. He said they probably wouldn't appreciate it and so I asked him why he was doing it. He leaned over real close to me and whispered in my ear. "Baseball," he said.

July 6

A man got lynched in Georgia yesterday. It wasn't in the white papers, but it was in the *World*. He was accused of attacking a white woman. When I read something like that it makes my stomach feel queasy.

Daddy belongs to the Elks, and they took up a collection for the family of the man who was killed. Daddy said that people feel sorry for the man who was killed, and that was right, but the people who were left behind suffered, too.

"It just drains you of any feeling that you're safe in the world," he said. "It makes you feel like you're nothing, just helpless to stand by and watch your people get killed."

That was the first time Daddy had said anything that made me think him and me were feeling the exact same thing.

July 7

We played in a triple-header at Morehouse College in Atlanta. The first game was the Baltimore Elite Giants against Morehouse for seven innings. The second game was Morehouse against the Barons for seven innings. The last game was a night game with the Giants against us. Morehouse is a black college and pretty much a la-di-da school. They were supposed to have some cheerleaders from Spelman College, but when the girls showed up from that school they were very classy and didn't look like cheerleaders, they looked like schoolteachers.

Bill Greason told me to try out one of my lines on them. I gave them a look but I had already heard them talking and they were too smart for me. Also, I did not have a line.

I got to play in the game against Morehouse and made an error. There was a fly ball to me in right field, and I tried to nonchalant it and dropped it.

Piper got on my case real bad, even though it was just an exhibition game. He said I was trying to catch like Willie Mays. I said I wasn't, but I guess I really was. Willie's just about my age, and so it's hard not to think about him when I'm on the field. He makes everything look so easy, though.

Piper saying that to me made me feel bad.

We talked with some of the guys from Morehouse, and they speak well. You can see that they're the kind of guys the girls from Spelman will marry. I'd like to be like them, too.

We played against the Baltimore Elite Giants, and their pitcher was Joe Black. He struck out everybody on our team at least once. They have a good team. Slow Robinson is their catcher and he's good, and Joe Black is just about sensational. They beat us 4 to 0. Jimmy Gilliam, on their team, hit four doubles to right field. His fifth time up he hit a ball to center that looked like a sure hit, but Willie got it.

July 8

I was thinking a lot about Morehouse. I've never met guys like that, guys who think they're special and smart. I think I'm smart but I don't think I'm as smart as the guys from Morehouse. We had dinner in Atlanta with some guys from Morehouse and some Spelman girls. I got all tongue-tied and didn't get to say much. Pepper said that the girls from Spelman were stuck up. I disagree. These are young black people that I would like to be like.

July 10

Durham, North Carolina. They had a beauty contest before the game, and the Birmingham Black Barons were the judges. After we picked the girl we thought was the best-looking, there was a big fight. Perry said that we were just trying to pick the most white-looking girl, and Jay Wilson said he should shut up and stop trying to make trouble. The girl didn't look white to me.

We played the Carolina All-Stars, and they made nine errors and two just-about errors. After the game a guy named Chris Mills from the All-Stars came over and talked to Piper about the game. He said that it was a good game but that the All-Stars were a little off. Piper got mad — you could tell that by the way the veins in his neck were showing — but he didn't say anything.

I know what made Piper mad. All of a sudden everybody was looking at the Negro Leagues and wondering what we were about. Some people looked at us as if we were a minor league, but our guys were as much of a major league as the National or the American League.

July 11

A doubleheader against the Carolina All-Stars, and Piper wanted to run the score on them but the team wasn't interested. We won both games (we didn't want Piper to blow up completely), but it was no big deal.

We saw an accident and stopped the bus. A car and a truck crashed just outside of Durham. There was white guy in the truck, and a black guy with a black girl in the car. The girl was hurt pretty bad, and so was the white guy. There was a little black hospital right near the accident, and they took them both there. If it had been a white hospital they would not have taken the black girl there.

July 12

We played a game against an industrial league team from Wilmington, North Carolina, and they were pretty good. Afterward we drove to a dinner where Buck Leonard was being honored. Everybody was asking Buck if he thought he would be playing white folks ball soon. Buck shrugged and said he was going to be forty-one in September. He said he had already had his time playing baseball.

It was real sad the way he said it, and you could tell that a lot of guys were thinking that maybe they wouldn't have a chance to play in the white leagues, either.

July 13

A day off.

July 17

In Cleveland against the Buckeyes. Sam Jethroe played center field and he looked 101 times better than Willie, who was playing center field for us. The thing with Willie is that when he's in the field he takes off as soon as the ball is hit. I don't know how he does that. I have to watch to see where the ball is going first and then I go after it. Willie's a pretty nice guy and always up for a ball game. He wants to play ball all the time. I think that's why Piper likes him. He's hitting pretty good, too.

July 18

Doubleheader against the Buckeyes. We won the first, and they won the second. I called home, and Mama answered the phone. She sounded kind of sad, and when I asked her what was wrong she said that Daddy wasn't laid off but they cut his hours back at the plant. I asked her if Daddy was down, and she said no, but he wasn't walking around doing no whole lot of grinning, either.

I told Mama about seeing the young people from Morehouse, and she said that I should apply if I wanted to go there.

Mama didn't push it, and neither did I. It takes money to go to college. I was giving Mama some of the money I was making from the Barons and I wasn't home eating all the time, so things weren't too bad there. Daddy made pretty good money when the hours were regular, but I knew Rachel would be going to school for a long time. Besides all that I didn't have a burning desire to be a teacher or a preacher or anything. I want to play ball, and later, when my career is over, I want to have a nice job that isn't just a job for a black man. I told Mama that I loved her and told her to tell Daddy that I loved him. She asked me was anything wrong and I said no, I was just thinking about some things.

July 19

Indianapolis. The bus halfway broke down, which meant that we had to crawl along the highway. It kept overheating, and the engine kept cutting off. The radiator was boiling off water as fast as we put it in, and Charlie said that we needed some oil. He didn't want to drive the bus to the next service station, and the guys didn't want to get off and walk. We ended up with Charlie driving along the highway slower than a guy walking. A police car came along, and the officer inside asked what the trouble was. Charlie told him, and he said we either had to put on some speed or get out and walk.

We said okay, but when the policeman left we kept starting and stopping the bus some more. It took us thirty minutes to make the five miles to the next service station, and guess who was sitting in the service station when we got there? That's right, the policeman. Charlie told him that the bus had started and was running just fine but had stopped a few minutes before we reached the service station.

The policeman asked Charlie if he was lying, and when Charlie said yes he got a ticket.

The gas station didn't have a Colored rest room, and the policeman (white) said that if anybody took out anything to pee on the highway, he was going to shoot off whatever we were going to pee with.

July 21

We played a game in Charleston, South Carolina, against the New York Cubans, who were traveling around the south. They were up first, and their third baseman, a guy named Minnie Minoso, bunted and got to first base, but the umpire called the ball foul. Minoso got mad and started yelling at the umpire but he was yelling in Spanish, and the umpire threw him out of the game. Their manager ran out and asked the umpire what Minoso was saying, and he said he didn't know but it sure didn't sound like Bible verses. It was only an exhibition game, and

Piper wanted to see Minoso play, so he talked to the umpire and got Minoso back in. Then Minoso hit three home runs to beat us 7 to 2, and Piper (surprise!) was mad.

After the game we went over to the black part of town and met a man who was one hundred years old. He looked it, too. He was small, and as black as you figure a man could get. The people from Charleston said he had been born a slave. I did some quick arithmetic and figured the man had to be born in 1848 if he was a hundred years old.

Bill Greason got to talking to him, and he told us a story about the Civil War. He said he and his cousin had both been drummer boys with the Colored troops during the war. He said they had all white Yankee officers who drilled them from sunup until sundown. They had a couple of skirmishes with the Rebs before they got into a big fight. In one fight the Rebs sent some dogs after them. He said that nearly scared the black off of him.

The Colored soldiers shot the dogs and then they turned and started shooting at the Rebs. Some of the Rebs would just stand up and yell at them, like they were back on the plantation and the Rebs were Patty Rollers. I asked him what a Patty Roller was, and he said they were white men who used to ride around the edge of the plantation to make sure nobody was stealing off.

He said once they were taken down to the beach and told they were going to attack a place called Fort Wagner.

There were supposed to be close to two hundred Rebs in there, and at least three times more Colored troops.

The old man had a tough-looking beard that was yellow and bristly, and he pulled on it faster and faster as he talked. He said those Colored soldiers lined up on the beach, and he and his cousin and a gap-toothed boy from Tennessee started beating their drums as they were told to do and then there was a charge. Instead of a couple of hundred Rebs in the fort there was near on to a thousand, or so it seemed, all waiting with their bayonets.

He said the Colored troops were beat back and some of their best officers killed, but they had proved something that day. They had proved the Colored soldier was a real fighter.

I was glad to see that old man, but it was amazing in a way, too. Here it is a hundred years later and we are still talking about how Jackie Robinson is proving that Colored people are okay at something. I told that to Bill Greason. He said if it didn't knock me down to the ground it meant I was getting stronger. I don't feel stronger.

July 22

Indianapolis, Indiana. We arrived at 1:30 p.m. and my back is just about broken from riding all night. Sam Hairston of the Clowns said that they had three games cancelled so far this month. A couple of their players said they were thinking of joining the army. Here is the current standing of the Negro American League:

Kansas City
Birmingham Black Barons
Memphis
Cleveland
Chicago
Indianapolis

Artie Wilson is the top hitter on the team. He's hitting .400, according to the *World*, but Artie said he was really hitting about .350.

The *World* gets its statistics from the team, but sometimes we forget to turn them in or somebody misplaces them.

They have a nice five-and-dime store in Indianapolis, and John Britton bought a statue of the Eiffel Tower for his mother and I bought one for Mama. One day I would like to go to Paris, where the real Eiffel Tower is. After the game (which we won 5 to 4) we went to a restaurant with some of the Clowns. I sat with Willie Mays, Bill Greason, and Luis Caballero of the Clowns.

After we had dinner, me and Willie walked around Indianapolis. We stopped at a coffee shop downtown and sat down at the counter and each of us had a soda. It was good not to have to look around to see if they had any WHITE and COLORED signs.

July 23

Willie got a humongous home run against Newark. The Eagles, which is what the Newark players are called, say they don't play nearly as many games as we do. The Barons play somewhere every day, but the Eagles say there aren't many teams to play up in the New Jersey area. The Eagles play their regular league games and a few games against Jersey City, and an occasional game out on Long Island, but they aren't drawing crowds.

Piper threw us a copy of the *World*, which had a big headline about Jackie Robinson and a small article about the Barons. There was also a lot of coverage of the Olympics, which are coming up pretty soon.

July 24

Home again and trouble. Daddy's job is still cutting back hours. What he does is work in a machine tool company. His job is to clean the metal shavings out of the machine and to keep them oiled.

They had laid off some of the guys who worked on the lathes and when they did that, everybody else got their hours cut.

Mama has been talking about getting a new sewing machine and she told Daddy that she needed it because Rachel was down to next to nothing for clothes. He told Mama to take her down to the New Ideal and buy her one of those fancy dresses that the white girls wear.

Aunt Jack asked Daddy what he was doing looking at what the white girls were wearing, but Mama said she didn't care what the white girls were wearing. A lot of the fancier white stores would not let black people try on the dresses, and if they did not fit when you got it home you could not take them back, either.

Mama said maybe she would take Rachel over to Miss Pool, who used to make her dresses.

"She still got that little piece of fake hair on her head?" Aunt Jack asked.

Mama said she did, but then she went on about how she needed to have her own sewing machine.

Rachel came in and started talking about how she wanted a store-bought dress, and Aunt Jack said that Rachel reminded her of an oxtail in a butcher's shop. She said she was probably good for seasoning something, but not for much more. I liked that.

July 25

Me and Rachel got into hot water and had the most fun we have had together in years. It all started at church this morning when there was a funeral. Mama said that Elder Lucas, who died last Wednesday, had not wanted to have his funeral on a Sunday, but the folks at Smith and Gaston Funeral Parlor were going on vacation the next day and so they had to have it right then. Daddy said Elder Lucas should have fixed it so he could have died on a Sunday, and then they could have buried him during the week. Mama got mad about that and said that he should not speak ill of the dead. Then Daddy said, "Humph!" Then Mama said not to be "humphing" her. Daddy said he was grown and he would "humph" who he wanted to. Then Mama "humphed" him, and he gave her two back. Just about that time I cracked up and so did Rachel, and we were both chased out of the kitchen.

July 25, night

We lost a doubleheader to the Newark Eagles. That's three out of four games we've lost against them. Jimmy Newberry came into the clubhouse and told Piper that one of the white owners of Rickwood wanted to see him right away. As soon as Piper left, the rest of us sneaked out because we didn't want to hear his mouth about losing the doubleheader.

Also, I got into a regular league game against Newark. Right after Monte Irvin put the game out of reach for us, Piper put me in. I got to bat against their relief pitcher, who is right-handed. He threw a ball sidearmed, and I jumped back from it just as the umpire called strike one. Then I stood in for the second pitch, which I really didn't see, and that was strike two. I missed the next pitch. Jimmy Zapp said that I looked like a southern white lady fanning herself. It made me feel bad because Willie Mays came up right after me and got a line drive single.

July 26

The big news is that President Truman has issued an order to integrate the armed forces. Everybody is talking about how that might mean the end of having to sit in the back of the bus or drink from a dirty drinking fountain under a COLORED sign. Most of the talk about how things are going to change is coming from young people. Older people say they'll just wait and see what happens.

Memphis is in town. The guys on the team were talking about the reports that the attendance was dropping off at the games. Piper said that the trouble with the black community is that we pay too much attention to what white people are doing.

Even the *Birmingham World* is just writing about what Jackie Robinson and Campanella and Doby are doing in the big leagues. I sent a scorecard to the *World*, but they didn't even print it.

We went over to Bob's Savoy, and the team had dinner together. Mr. Hayes, the team owner, came by and told us that he was proud of us and that no matter what happened, we were representing the Negro Leagues well.

Bobby Robinson is back and he asked Piper who was going to be playing in center field. He said he needed to get some game time now that his broken leg was healed. Willie Mays was right there when he asked, and Piper looked Bobby right in the face and said that Willie had earned the job and that Bobby was going to have to earn it back. This didn't set well with Bobby, and he told Piper that he was just letting Willie play because he knew Cat, Willie's father. Piper said that he had made this decision and he didn't care who liked it.

Later, when we were getting the equipment on the team bus, I asked Piper if he was mad at Bobby or something. Piper said he wasn't mad at Bobby but that as fast as Bobby was, Willie was even faster and had a better throwing arm. He said he wasn't even mad at Bobby for what he said about him playing Willie because he knew his father.

We got out to Rickwood, and there was a big crowd of white people there. Usually there were some white people at the baseball games, but now that Negroes were going up and playing white folks ball, more of them were showing up. It soon got around that Satchel Paige was in the crowd, and he was.

Now that was a funny thing to me. Because Satchel was always a star in our league, but nobody went as crazy over him as they did now he was in the major leagues. He was Satchel and he was a good ballplayer and a good entertainer. People came to see him a lot, but they didn't go crazy over him. But now that he was playing white folks ball with Cleveland, people were wanting to take a good look at him.

Before the game Satchel came down to the dugouts. He was wearing this big brimmed hat and wore a pinkie ring on his pitching hand. Artie Wilson asked Satch how come he wasn't with the Indians, and Satch said he had to go and have a meeting with the commissioner.

He took out a clipping, and we read it. It was the same story that I had read in the *Birmingham World*. The baseball commissioner had said that Satch's hesitation pitch was illegal.

Okay, the thing was that Satch could deliver the ball. It was on you like a heartbeat. But Satch is tall, and his windup is slow, so you watch him and watch him and then *zip*, the ball is past you. That's what he does normally. But with the hesitation pitch he starts his windup, you get your body all ready to swing, and then he stops. When he hesitates like that, you relax a second and then he whips the ball in. By the time you tense up enough to get some muscle on your swing, the ball is on you and you're lucky if you get a foul tip.

We went out and played five good innings against Memphis with Powell pitching. Powell even tried Satch's hesitation pitch and hit Willie Wells, Jr., on the elbow. Willie used some language I didn't know he even knew. Piper was mad, too. He went out and stood on the foul line and just stared at Powell. When the inning was over he took Powell out and put in Heard. Heard gave up four quick runs, and the game was just about over.

After the game Satch came into the locker room and asked if anybody could give him a lift to the train station. He had to go meet the Indians at their next stop.

On the trains there were cars for white people, and cars for black people once the trains got to the south, the same as there were "white" waiting rooms and "Colored" waiting rooms. When there were laws that separated the races like that, we called them "Jim Crow" laws, and when

Joe Scott asked Satch 'if he had to ride in the Jim Crow car, we all knew what he was talking about.

Satch was straightforward about it. He said he and Doby didn't have to move out of the white cars because the team took up the whole car, but they couldn't eat in the dining room. They had to eat in the kitchen with the Negro porters. But everybody knew that was where the good food was served.

Willie Mays said he wouldn't ride in the Jim Crow car, even if he was going through the south. Bobby asked him if he could turn invisible and said if he couldn't he would have his butt in the Jim Crow car like everybody else.

July 27

Got home and Daddy was sleeping in his overalls on the couch and Mama and Aunt Jack were having coffee in the kitchen. I thought I heard Mama crying, but I'm not sure. It was past midnight, and so I think something is up. Rachel came to my room and asked me if it was true that Satchel Paige was at the ballpark. I said no. If I'd said yes, I would have had to tell her what he was wearing, what he said, and who said what to him. I didn't want to get into all that, so I just said no. She said she didn't believe me, and I told her to shut up and go to bed. She slammed the door shut, and I started to jump up and make her come back and shut it right, but I don't like to mess with Rachel because she always gets you back.

July 28

We were sitting around having breakfast, and I saw everybody was upset. Daddy making believe he's reading the paper, and Mama making believe she's reading the Bible. In our family Aunt Jack is the Bible reader, but Mama was sitting there looking in the carrying Bible, the one we carry to church, and humming to herself.

Aunt Jack had made grits, eggs, and bacon. It was real bacon, not just strick-o-lean, too. We all ate in silence, and the food was hard going down.

Mama wanted to buy a sewing machine and some other things but she didn't want to take money out of the bank to do it, so she wanted to get a job. There had been a lot of jobs for black men and women during the war, but once the war ended and all the white soldiers came home, jobs were not that easy to find, especially for black women.

Mama was saying that work was work and it did not make that much difference what she did as long as it was not against the law or against the church. Daddy did not see things that way. Most of the jobs around Birmingham for black women were domestic jobs, and Daddy did not want Mama working for Miss Ann, which is what he called white women.

Daddy said that before the war half the black women who worked in Birmingham worked in the home of a white person, cooking and cleaning, or taking care of their children. It was not so hard a job as it was a "place" kind of thing. It seemed like it was the black woman's "place" to be working for the white woman.

In some ways things looked pretty good for black people. Some of our ballplayers were going into the major leagues, and with the armed forces integrating, a lot of people thought our lives were going to change in a big way. But if you were black and did not have your own business or a professional job like teaching, preaching, or undertaking, you were always just one argument or one slowdown from having to beg somebody to let you make a decent living.

Rachel told me later that she thought Daddy was wrong. I kind of thought he was wrong, too, but I knew how he felt.

August 2

Monday, and we are home for two days. We lost a doubleheader yesterday against the Monarchs. We were up against Mickey Stubblefield in the first game, and Piper said we should have hit him but we didn't. We were behind 5 to 2 in the ninth, and he got Ed Steele, Jimmy Zapp, and Willie Mays on four pitches. Pepper said they were freezing the balls, which meant that they were packing them in ice the night before. When they pack the balls in ice, it takes the life out of them. You can hit a ball smack on the button and it won't go anywhere.

The second game was pitched by Greason for us and Jim LaMarque for the Monarchs. The game was scoreless in the sixth inning, when LaMarque got tired and loaded up the bases on three straight walks with no outs. Then Hilton Smith came in and struck out three men in a row, including Piper.

In the bottom of the seventh, Buck O'Neil hit a high drive to right field, which everybody thought was going to be a home run. He was jogging around the bases, but the ball hit the wall and stayed in. Willie got it and almost threw Buck out at second base. Piper was pretty happy about that. Then Elston Howard got up and hit a low line drive into center, and Willie came in, got the ball on a short hop, and held Buck on third. Piper was happy about that, too. Then Hank Thompson hit a line drive into the left-field bleachers. That ball got into the bleachers so fast, I couldn't believe it. Guess who was mad?

On the way back to Birmingham the bus was quiet. There weren't even any card games.

August 3

Mama and Daddy have still been at it. Aunt Jack said she would cash in her burial insurance to buy Mama the sewing machine she wanted. Mama said that Aunt Jack could not do that because it would be shame if something happened to her when she didn't have burial insurance. Daddy was mad, too.

Aunt Jack said it didn't make any difference what happened to her when she was dead because her soul was right with God. Then she said she did not want to see a family in turmoil because of a sewing machine, and Mama got mad about that and said that she only had one good nerve left and Aunt Jack was working it down to a nub.

I was not even thinking when I said that I would buy Mama the sewing machine. She gave me a big hug and a kiss. That settled things for a while, but then when I was packing my bag to go to the ballpark Daddy came in and asked if I thought I had done the right thing. I said, yes, I did. He said he thought it was the right thing, too, but that I should have done it a lot sooner and that maybe I had forgotten that we were family. Him saying that got my jaw tight, but I just left it in the corner.

August 4

Chicago and Quincy Trouppe and the Chicago American Giants. We went to a restaurant in the Colored section, and it was the fanciest I have ever been in. It's the size of Bob's Savoy in Birmingham but a lot fancier. All of their waitresses were light-skinned, and Bill Greason said that the owners were color-struck. At the restaurant were Piper, Bill Greason, me, Quincy Trouppe, Mel Carter from the Giants, and a white man named Mr. Leonard Chance. That's what he called himself — Mr. Leonard Chance. He was an agent for the major leagues.

Piper asked him what team he was scouting for, and he said he was not scouting for a particular team, just looking around for likely players so that he could make his services available to the major leagues. Bill asked him what he meant by "likely."

Mr. Chance started talking about speed, size, and strength. He also said that they were looking for Negroes with good character, not men living the fast life. He was not interested in drinkers or men who liked the ladies too much, or gamblers.

That sounded okay to me, but Bill Greason got mad. Later, when we got back to the hotel we were staying in, I asked him why he was mad. He said that the way Mr. Chance was talking, it was like he was looking for slaves.

Bill said about a third of our players could play in the major leagues the next day. By letting in just a few at a time they could pick and choose who they took and then make the ones they took jump through hoops to stay. I thought about what that old man in Charleston had said about the Colored troops proving themselves at Fort Wagner.

August 5

We played against Chicago again, but this time we played in Rockford, Illinois. Rockford is a quiet little town, and I liked it. White folks brought us fried chicken and potato salad, and we were invited to their church services this Sunday, but we'll be back in Birmingham by then. Sam Hill, the Giants center fielder, spiked Artie Wilson at second base, and Artie and him got into a pushing match. The umpire broke up the fight and threw Artie out of the game. Piper said that if they threw Artie out, the Barons were going to leave. Quincy Trouppe spoke to the umpire, and Artie stayed in the game.

It's always the outfielders spiking people. That's because they don't play on the bases and don't know what it's like to have some spikes headed toward your face. The pitcher is the only one who can get back at an outfielder.

When Hill got up the next inning, Alonzo Perry hit him with the first pitch. Perry is tall and got nine kinds of angles on him so if he throws the ball up you don't know where it's going. Then when he hits you he gives you a mean look, and you know that he would not mind hitting you again.

I asked Piper if he was ever afraid to get hit by the ball. He said it did not bother him at all, that he liked to have a few knots upside his head because it made combing his hair interesting. I didn't think he had to say all that.

August 6

Birmingham. We're playing the Harlem Globetrotters later tonight in a nonleague game. Guess who's pitching for them now? Joe Bankhead. Piper says if he pitches against us we're going to knock him from here to Seattle, Washington, and make him wish he was playing for the House of David.

The House of David was a white team. They all wore beards but they could play ball. Piper didn't like playing ball against any team that did anything different, because it was not "pure" ball. They were one of the few white teams we played, and we couldn't play against them in the south.

August 7

We played Cleveland and beat Sad Sam Jones. The whole team came together, and it was a good feeling. Being at Rickwood, being back in Birmingham, and playing in front of our fans made everything all right. A whole bunch of guys from H. Y. Carson Plating came to the game. Johnny Britton's cousin works there and he came over and took some pictures with the team.

Willie Mays had a good game, but Bobby Robinson is mad because he wants to play and Piper is still going with Willie. Piper told Bobby he would let him play against Baltimore. Bobby's brother, "Slow" Robinson, caught for the Baltimore Elite Giants.

Word came down that Piper Davis, Bill Powell, and Artie Wilson had made the All-Star team. Pepper said they must have paid somebody off. Wiley Griggs said that Pepper couldn't buy his way onto an All-Monkey team. He thought that was pretty funny until Pepper threw his catcher's mask and hit him in the face.

Piper fined both of them fifteen dollars, and Pepper said he wouldn't pay it.

August 8

Doubleheader against Cleveland. Before the game I went out to the outfield and caught a few balls. It's a good feeling. The grass in Rickwood looks greener, the dirt is dark and kind of reddish, and the sky today was bluer than it has been for a long time. The crowd wasn't that big but it was loud, and all rooting for us. We took both games from the Buckeyes with Powell pitching the first game like he was proud to make the All-Star team.

The second game was a runaway. Even Willie got two hits. When Piper let me bat in the bottom of the sixth against Brewer, I was real anxious to get a hit. Nothing. I didn't even see his fastball. He called up to the plate and told me where he was going to pitch the ball, but I couldn't catch up to it.

I love this game, but it don't love me.

August 9

We have a game in Mobile, Alabama, against the Cleveland Buckeyes. The site of the game was not decided until the last minute, so we had to hustle to get to Mobile and when two of the Cleveland cars broke down, half of them rode with us, which was fun because they clown around a lot. We stopped to get some lunch at a white diner, mostly hamburgers and frankfurters and bottles of pop. When we got to the ballpark we found that a couple of the players weren't there. Just before the game started, Sam Williams showed up and said that Herman Bell had been arrested.

Sam did not know why Bell had been arrested. He had been buying a newspaper and when he turned around he saw two policemen putting Bell into the back of a police car.

Piper called me over and told me to get Charlie. I got Charlie, and we got into the bus and went into town. We found the sheriff's office and went in. Soon as we walked in and they saw the uniforms, the sheriff asked what us "boys" wanted.

We told him and found out that Bell had been arrested for disturbing the peace. We got to go to the back of the station where the cells are and found Bell sitting in one of them with a towel over his eye. Piper asked him what happened and said he saw a big stray dog drinking out of one of the "white" water fountains and thought it was funny. He was taking a picture of it when the sheriff came over and arrested him. I asked him what happened to his eye.

Bell looked at the deputy and then said he had slipped on his way to jail.

It cost us twenty dollars to get Bell out of jail. On the bus headed toward the stadium, Bell started crying. Piper asked him if he was hurting and he said no, that he wasn't. Then Piper didn't say anything more, and neither did anyone else. I knew Bell was hurting inside.

August 11

Three games against the Asheville Blues. Piper says that he's sure the Monarchs are going to win the second half. He doesn't know if they're playing to get into the Negro League World Series or if they're playing to impress the white scouts.

We beat Asheville easily. They only got one good hit when one of their players, a guy called Big Cat Brown, got a smash into deep left center. Willie couldn't catch up with it, and when it got through for a hit the Asheville player started into his home-run trot. Willie ran the ball down, threw it in to Artie Wilson, and they cut the guy down at the plate.

August 13

Yesterday was my birthday. We hooked up with Baltimore in Monroe, Louisiana. Monroe is so hot that you can't walk more than a few steps without the sweat pouring down. Piper let Bobby Robinson play so he could play against his brother, and that got Willie Mays mad. This is how the game went:

First inning: They got one run off of Sam Williams, and we got nothing off Joe Black. Second inning: They got one run off Sam Williams, and we got nothing off Joe Black. Third inning: They got two runs off Sam Williams, and Sam Williams got taken out of the game. We got nothing off Joe Black. Piper told Sam Williams that he was fired from the Black Barons.

Fourth inning: They got nothing off Bill Powell, and Joe Black put us down one two three.

Fifth inning: They got three straight singles off Powell, and Piper signaled me to bring out some water. When I got out to the mound with the water, Piper was asking Powell what was wrong with him and Powell said he thought he was having a heatstroke. Piper told him he could have as many heatstrokes he wanted to have after the game. They ended up with two more runs that inning. The final score of the game was 11 to 1. Okay, then the guys from Baltimore started laughing at us and saying things like we needed to go back to Birmingham and play against some of the high school players because we weren't ready for no big leagues. That made everybody mad. Charlie Rudd just shook his head and walked off.

Piper was mad and yelling at me, and anybody else that got near him.

I got the stuff on the bus, and all the players piled on. They had bought some beer and sandwiches from a Colored store and started eating as soon as they got on the bus. Piper told Charlie to get going because we had to go all the way to Savannah. Charlie kept fooling around, and Piper was getting on his case and Charlie pointed across the parking lot and said he just wanted to see something.

We looked over at the Baltimore bus, and they were getting out of it. The driver lifted the hood and was scratching his head. Pepper said he wasn't going to give them a hand. Charlie said they didn't need a hand, what they needed was a distributor cap, and he tossed the one he had taken from their engine out the window.

August 16

Two industrial league teams came in from Mobile, Alabama, and we played five innings against each of them. They had this kid who was batboy for both teams. He was only fourteen and he took a few swings at batting practice. The kid — he's got two first names, Hank and Aaron — didn't know how to hold the bat. He's right-handed but he held the bat with his left hand on top of his right hand. I told him he'd probably break his wrists that way, but he kept on doing it. Not too bright.

In the middle of the second five-inning game they announced over the loudspeaker that Babe Ruth had died, and asked everybody to stand for a moment of silence. It was a sad thing and affected all the players. When a baseball player died, especially a great player like Babe Ruth, it was like somebody in your family died.

August 17

We played a doubleheader against the New York Cubans at Rickwood. Charlie Richards was at the game and sat in our dugout. The Cubans had a lot of Spanish ballplayers and they used to shout around the infield in Spanish. They could play, too. Their infield was as slick as anything with Lorenzo Cabrera on first base, Pedro Miro on second, Miguel "Pedro" Ballestro at shortstop, and Minnie Minoso on third. If you hit a ball in the infield you could forget it because they were going to gobble it up and throw you out.

We split the doubleheader with the Cubans. Piper had taken out the regulars for the second game. He said it was clear we weren't going to win both halves of the season, so we were going to be in a play-off and he wanted everybody healthy.

August 18

Greensboro, North Carolina. A nice town. Bill Greason said he loved to play baseball on a warm Sunday afternoon. Perry reminded him that it was Wednesday, not Sunday.

Bill said he was twenty-three, had ten dollars in his pocket, and the Lord loved him, so it had to be Sunday.

We won an exhibition against a Greensboro team. The field we were playing on was so hard that there were a lot of errors made.

Artie Wilson said there was a big difference in the way you play when you were playing in a place like Comiskey Park or Yankee Stadium every day. The grounds in those places were always level, and you did not have to worry about the ball hitting a pebble or a hard patch of ground and bouncing over your glove. He said some of the white guys from the major leagues would not even think of playing on some of the fields we made a living on.

August 22

Against the New York Cubans at New Orleans. We split with them again. Then some of the Cubans took us out to eat in a little restaurant that made what they called Creole food. I had white bean soup, kale, and chicken gumbo over red rice. It was about three kinds of good, but I almost messed it up. All the Spanish guys put hot sauce on their food, and so I put some on mine. That food must have already been hot because with that sauce on it I liked to have keeled over and died! The second plate was better.

After we ate we went to a party, and I thought some of the girls there were white but they weren't, just the most light-skinned Negro girls I have ever seen. I got to thinking about what Mama had said about "road girls" and I would not have minded if one of them got their hands on Yours Truly.

August 25

New York City! The All-Star game. I am writing this in a hotel in which both black and white people stay. After a day back home the guys who made the All-Star team got a lift up to New York from Neil Robinson of the Memphis Red Sox. I asked Piper if I could come along, and he said yes since he didn't have to pay my way.

Bill Powell started the game for our team (the West), which made me feel very proud. Then Jim LaMarque from the Monarchs came on for us, and Gentry Jessup finished the game. The East team got three measly hits! Minnie Minoso got one, Buck Leonard got one, and

Jimmy Gilliam from Baltimore got one. We got seven hits, including a double by Piper. The official attendance for the game was 42,000, but everyone said there were probably closer to 50,000 people in the stands. Some people said that the game was the best they had ever seen! It was one of the best games I had ever seen, and the players knew it. Every swing was a little more determined, and every throw was a little harder. The final score was the West (with three Black Barons) 3, and the East a big fat 0!

After the game there was a party at a restaurant near Yankee Stadium. Most of the ballplayers were there, and some of their wives. Some white ballplayers were there, and there were a lot of white scouts, too. The scouts were talking to all the ballplayers and asking them what team they played for.

When the party with all the white people was over, some of the black players went outside and took taxis to Harlem. We were all dressed in street clothes but when we went into a place called The Showcase, some people still recognized Piper and Quincy Trouppe and knew we were in town for the All-Star game. They came over and shook our hands and stuff. Real good.

The Showcase is a little like Bob's Savoy. They have a dance floor and a band and everything. The people there were dressed better than anything I had ever seen in Birmingham. Everybody was feeling good until Tommy

Louden (of the New York Cubans) said something about maybe by the next year all the All-Stars would be in the major leagues and playing white folks ball. Some of the players said they would sure like to get some of that white folks money and they were talking about how it would be easier to play in the major leagues than it was in the Negro Leagues.

Luke Easter said, white folks will never really understand what the Negro Leagues were like unless they played against the whole league instead of just taking some players. He said people see a handful of players who are around now but they had never seen people like Oscar Charleston, or Luis Tiant, or Cool Papa Bell when they were in their prime. All they knew about Satchel Paige was that he can compete against big-league players, Easter said. They had not seen him when he was young and could throw a BB through a straw.

I would have liked to have seen Satch in his twenties and throwing as hard as everybody was talking about. I would also have liked to have stayed up all night and just walked around Harlem, looking at everything, but Piper went back to the hotel and I went with him, only now I'm too excited to sleep.

August 31

The season is just about over. We're not going to catch the Monarchs and so we're going to have to face them in a play-off. Word is going around that the Newark Eagles have been sold to somebody in Texas.

September 5

This is the next-to-last day of the season, and we have just finished playing two games against the Red Sox here in Memphis. We won the first, and they won the second. The whole team is healthy, and Piper took out the regulars in the second game. I thought he might put me in, but he didn't. I was going to ask him if he thought I wasn't good enough to play baseball in this league, but I didn't. I think I know the answer. It doesn't matter; I still love the game and I'll play whenever I can.

Sam Lacy, a reporter, was around interviewing people. He is smooth and speaks well. That's something I would like to do: write about sports.

September 8

We're going to play the Monarchs in the play-offs starting this Saturday. The first game will be at Rickwood. We had a team meeting at Bob's Savoy, and Mr. Hayes, the team's owner, asked us how we were going to do. Jimmy Zapp stood up and said we were going to win the play-offs and then destroy whoever won the East. The East will be between the Homestead Grays and the Baltimore Elite Giants. If I bet, I would sure put my money on the Grays.

I told Mama that maybe I wouldn't stay with the team next year. I told her it was a real job and everything but maybe I would apply for a job at the steel mill. She asked me if that was the only job I was interested in. Charlie Richards was going into the navy, and I thought maybe I would go in with him. Mama said she'd hate to see me go a long way from home. She teared up a little, and I knew she did not want me to go into the navy.

Later, after supper, all of us were sitting out on the front porch listening to the radio. Daddy was sitting in his undershirt and leaning against the rail with his eyes kind of closed. Aunt Jack asked if anybody wanted some peach cobbler, and we all said yes. When she went in to get it, Mama went with her and that left just me and Daddy and Rachel on the porch.

Daddy asked me how I liked my first season with the Black Barons, and I told him I liked it just fine but I was not sure what was going to happen next year. He asked me if I had given any more thought to going to college, and I said I had. Nobody in our family has been to college,

Daddy said. He asked me if I thought it was time for somebody to go, and when I said yes, he got up, stretched his back, and then said that if I wanted to go to college he would find a way of paying for it.

Later I was lying in bed thinking about what Daddy had said when Rachel knocked on my door and came in. She said if I did not go to college I should go to undertaking school because people were dying all the time and my customers would not mind my bad breath. She actually thought that was funny enough to come all the way to my room to tell it to me.

September 11

Things have changed a lot since I wrote last. All the talk at home is about me going to college. Mr. Parrish, Rachel's piano teacher, knows the registrar at Talladega College and he called him to talk about me. The registrar wanted to know if I was interested in coaching their baseball team. Yes, I am! They would give me a scholarship to the school in return for me working with their baseball team.

The first thing in the morning, before sunrise, Skeeter, the dog I got from Pijo King, started barking. Mama came and told me to go downstairs to see what the problem was. I didn't see any problem and tried to put Skeeter outside, but he wouldn't go. He kept barking at the couch. Then Daddy came down and told me to get him and put him out, and I went to get him and just as I did a squirrel ran from behind the couch and up the stairs. Skeeter ran after him, and a hot second later the squirrel came down the stairs and me and Daddy chased it until it jumped out of an open window. Well, Daddy thought that was the funniest thing and laughed like crazy. When Mama came down and saw him laughing like that, she went over and kind of leaned against him and he put his arm around her. Nice.

September 11, night

I am so tired, I cannot see straight. Rickwood was jammed today with both white and black fans. The *Birmingham News* carried a big story about the team and wished us luck. The team met at the Savoy, and Mr. Hayes went around shaking everybody's hand.

He said that all the owners in the league respect our team because of the way we play, the way we conduct ourselves off the field, and the way we respect the fans.

That made me feel good, but I knew the Monarchs, who had won the second half of the season, weren't going to be a pushover. We had to meet them in the league play-off, and then whoever won was in the Negro League World Series. Kansas City was a good baseball town, the same as Birmingham, and they were proud of their team, too.

By the time we got to the stadium for the first play-off game, my stomach was in knots. Piper saw that I was nervous and he said not to worry about it, that we had to turn our nervousness into action.

The first game was hard and everyone was nervous, but we were playing well. The Monarchs' infield was knocking down every ball hit their way and throwing our runners out. LaMarque pitched for them and was stingy with his hits at first, but then we got to him. They came right back, and by the ninth inning the score was tied. The Barons came up in the last of the ninth with a chance to win it, but the Monarchs held on. Missing that chance got to me, and I had to go in the clubhouse and use the bathroom.

In the top of the tenth we got them out, and I breathed a sigh of relief, as did the rest of the team.

The bottom of the tenth and Piper smashed a hit to left center. Johnny Britton grounded out to first, but Piper moved on to second. Ed Steele got up and hit two bodacious fouls down the right field line. The next ball was way outside and Piper started to go, changed his mind, and then had to scramble back to second. The next ball to Ed Steele looked high, and I think Ed wanted to just foul it off to be sure but he popped it up behind the plate. Two outs.

Pepper was up next and he swung and missed two straight curveballs. The next pitch was a fastball off the plate, and Pepper just did hold up his swing. The next ball was fast and inside and a little low. Then their pitcher threw a curve, and Pepper hit a line drive toward the right-field corner. Their right fielder cut it off on one bounce, but Piper was already rounding third and heading for the plate. By the time the ball got into the first baseman for the relay, Piper was on home plate. We won the game 5 to 4.

September 12

Sunday. Aunt Jack made sausages, eggs, and grits for breakfast. Rachel got into trouble, and I was on her side for a change. On Saturday afternoon she had put a lot of Dixie Peach hair pomade on her hair and left it on for a long time because her friend Irene told her that it would make her hair really silky. Then she went to comb it out with a hot comb and burned the back of her neck really bad. Mama made her put a bandage on the burn, and Rachel wanted to wear a bandanna around her neck to church.

Mama said she was not going to let Rachel go to church looking like a fast girl, so she could not wear the bandanna.

Rachel's neck was hurting, and she was feeling bad and I felt bad for her.

At church we sang "Precious Lord, Take My Hand," even though nobody had died.

September 12, second time

This was the best game I have ever seen in my whole life. The first few innings were scoreless, and things were tense. When Piper got up for his second at bat he hit a drive that shook up the entire stadium. Piper could hit, but he never hit that far before. The ball went over the scoreboard, which is 380 feet away. That scoreboard is thirty-three feet high!

I thought that was going to be the game, right then and there, but the Monarchs settled down, and by the ninth the score was 5 to 4, their favor. Willie Mays singled in the tying run in the bottom of the ninth and we won it in the bottom of the tenth! Whew!

September 15

The Monarchs' regular stadium was being used by another team, and so we played the next game at Martin Park in Memphis. Another tight game, but the score was tied when Jimmy Zapp came up to the plate in the ninth. We were all yelling for him to get something started. What he did was hit a pitch deep into the left-field stands. The Monarchs got one hit in the bottom of the ninth when Souell beat out a ball to deep short, but with two outs Willie Mays ran down a drive by Elston Howard to end the game. We were up three games to nothing. This series is going to be a lot easier than I thought!

September 19

We lost three games in a row. I can't believe it. The whole team was down when we got back to Birmingham. We got a lot of people talking to us and telling us we could still win, but I wasn't sure anymore. When the team got to Rickwood for the final game the stands were already starting to fill up, and by game time there was wall-to-wall people. We heard that there were people outside who couldn't get in.

The Dunbar High School band played "The Star-Spangled Banner," and the game started. When Charlie Richards came into our dugout and sat next to me I didn't want him to know how scared I was. The truth was I started off scared and got scareder when the Monarchs jumped out in front early. Bill Greason was pitching, and he's my man and I was nervous, especially since Jim LaMarque was pitching for the Monarchs. But that one run was all they got, and we took the game 5 to 1.

All the guys were screaming and shouting in the locker room. We were hugging each other and grinning all over the place. This is what I wanted, to be on a winning team and yell and slap everybody on the back.

A photographer took a bunch of pictures of us hugging each other and then a team picture of all the regulars. Talk about one great day! Talk about one great team!

September 25

The Homestead Grays played their home games at either Forbes Field in Pittsburgh or Griffith Stadium in Washington, D.C., but they couldn't get either of their home fields for the Negro League World Series because they were being used by major-league teams. That's why the first game of the series was going to be in Kansas City. We got to Muehlebach Field in Kansas City late Thursday afternoon, and Piper was so anxious to get the series started, he wanted to have a workout right away but we couldn't get anyone to open the stadium. Piper had faced the Homestead Grays in the Negro World Series in 1944 and 1945, and both times he lost. I knew he had those losses in the back of his mind.

Everybody wanted to win, and most of the guys were feeling good about our chances. Jimmy Newberry started for us and he looked good warming up.

The first inning went smoothly, with nobody scoring. But in the bottom of the second Newberry gave up a hit, and then walked the next batter. Wham! Wham! Before you knew it, they had three runs. When the team came in they were quiet, which is a bad sign.

Newberry had his head down, and a couple of guys went over to him and touched him on the shoulder. I went over to him, too.

The next inning he was throwing nothing but some heat and got the Grays out one two three. We started chipping away, a hit here, and a hit there, and went into the last two innings trailing by one run. We got a rally going in the eighth and got Pepper as far as third base, but he got thrown out when he tried to score on a groundout to third. They hadn't done squat against Newberry after the second inning, but we couldn't tie it up. After the game we were faced with an all-night ride back to Birmingham. It rained all the way, which seemed just about right.

September 26

Rachel put some mascara on, and it got in her eye and turned it all red. She told Mama she was getting a sty, but

Mama found the mascara in her room and said she shouldn't lie about it, especially on a Sunday.

Church started early today so everybody could go to the game. I wanted to pray for the Barons to win but I didn't think that was right. I did pray for Ed Steele to get a home run.

September 26, night

Second inning. Runners on first and third and Scott up. Bam! A double off the right-field wall. Both runners scored, and we're up 2 to 0 with Bill Powell pitching. Everything was great until the sixth inning. Then the Grays got five runs. They are one good-hitting ball club. Luke Easter hit a low outside pitch against the left-field wall. He's a huge dude and strong as skunk pee.

Piper got on in the ninth with one out. Bell pinch-hit and got a double, and Piper, who was running from the crack of the bat, scored to make it 5 to 3. But then Artie Wilson struck out, and Johnny Britton grounded out to Easter at first base. We lost 5 to 3, which put them two up.

September 28, midnight

Perry pitched and got a wicked double in the third inning to knock in a run. In the fourth inning who gets a home run for the Grays? Right, Luke Easter. Every time he gets up, I get nervous.

In the top of the sixth, with two outs, Buck Leonard is on first base. Clarence Bruce, who was playing second for the Grays, knocked the crap out of the ball into left center field for a base hit. Willie is out in center and he gets to the ball before it goes through to the wall. Leonard goes flying around second base and heads for third. Willie guns him down with a perfect throw to third. Couldn't believe it. Neither could Buck, who stood up and watched Willie come in from the outfield. He was shaking his head. Willie has some arm.

In the sixth inning we got the lead back. We got two hustle runs. A drag bunt down the first baseline, and a soft single to right field put two guys on. Then Zapp popped up for the first out, but Piper singled to drive in a run and put runners on first and third. A called third strike on Pepper made the second out, but Piper hustled down to second on a delayed steal. Then, on the next pitch, Eudie Napier, a really solid catcher for the Grays, let the ball get past him, and we scored our second run of the inning.

In the eighth inning they tied the score when Bob Thurman hit a two-run double.

Bottom of the ninth. One out. Bill Greason, who relieved Perry in the eighth inning, got a single. Art Wilson hit a short fly to center field. He slammed the bat down, but it was still the second out. Okay, who comes up but Willie. In the dugout nobody says anything. I sneaked a look over at Piper, who was sitting with his ankles crossed. I knew he was nervous.

Willie took the first pitch right down the middle for a strike. The next pitch was way high. The next was a curve, which Willie started to go for and stopped his bat. The umpire called it a strike.

It looked low to me.

The next pitch was fast and low, and Willie hit a wicked shot right over the mound. That ball went over second base and into center field. Greason scored, and we had our first win.

September 29

It's about three hundred miles from Birmingham to New Orleans, but it could have been nine hundred miles, we didn't care, we had won our first game.

Some of the Grays were mad that they had to play in New Orleans, because they couldn't play in front of the fans who had supported them most of the year. They were even madder when we got to Pelican Stadium in New Orleans.

When we played league games in the south, the audience wasn't segregated. When the white Barons played at

Rickwood, the stands would have a white section and a black section. In our league games most of the fans were black, and you could sit anywhere you wanted to sit. But when we got to Pelican Stadium, the owners decided that so many white fans were coming to the game that they were going to use the segregation rules. The black section of Pelican Stadium was divided from the white section by a wire fence.

Wilmer Fields was pitching for the Grays. He's a hard thrower but he usually doesn't have too much on his ball. Piper said we could hit him if we concentrated. What happened was that everybody on the Grays was on their game. They hit everything and everybody we put into the game. We didn't do a thing against Fields. We lost 14 to 1.

I felt bad for Piper. He wanted to win the series and I wanted to win the series, but it was looking bad.

Charlie Rudd took the bus down Canal Street before turning onto the highway. We wanted to leave Louisiana, and our loss, as fast as we could. A few black people saw the bus on the road and waved, but nobody felt like waving back.

October 1

We did our best. We played like champions, but it wasn't enough. We lost the fifth game, at home, in ten innings,

10 to 6. We've lost the series four games to one. I feel terrible.

October 2

Mr. Hayes gave a party at Rush's Hotel for the Black Barons and anyone in their families who wished to come. All of the Black Barons came, and some of the Homestead Grays who were still in town. Mama came, and Daddy came because he wanted to meet Buck Leonard. I introduced them, and Daddy shook Buck's hand and said that he was pleased to meet him.

Buck said that he was worried about winning the series until the last Baron was out. "You guys know how to play this game," he said.

Alonzo Perry asked me what I was going to do over the winter. He's tall and leaned over me when he talked. I told him I was thinking about going to college.

He told me that him, Willie Mays, Bobby Robinson, and Pepper were going to start driving down to Florida next week. He knew a guy down there who could hook them up with a team in Puerto Rico and wanted to know if I wanted to go with them.

It hurt me to say no, it really did. Maybe I will be all right at college, I don't know. I know I cannot play baseball well enough to be in the Negro Leagues.

I wasn't going to give baseball up, just the dream of being a professional. I would always root for the Black Barons and love watching them and being around them.

October 3

After church Aunt Jack and Mama were in the kitchen snapping beans for supper. Rachel was doing homework, and Daddy was sitting out on the front porch. I went out and sat with him. He asked me if I wanted to catch a few. He saw I was surprised and told me that he had his own glove somewhere in the shed out in back of the house. I said fine.

Daddy went to the shed and came back with the most raggedy glove I have ever seen in my life. It was so stiff from not having any oil on it for years that I could hardly get my hand in it. I got my glove, and we went into the backyard and started throwing the ball around. We had only been doing it for five minutes or so when Bill Greason came by. He watched us and smiled.

Rachel, who was watching us from the window, called down to Bill and asked him if he thought me and Daddy looked like ballplayers. Bill said we did and if a few more guys showed up it would be a perfect day for a double-header.

Epilogue

◆◆

After completing high school, Rachel Owens worked in a beauty parlor in Birmingham. Noticing that there were few cosmetics designed for black women, she started a company that manufactured face powders, lipsticks, and other cosmetics. She married Frank Lopez, an accountant. The couple had two children, a boy and a girl. The boy was one of the children injured when racists bombed the Sixteenth Street Baptist Church in 1963. Presently Rachel spends her time flying around the country promoting her company's products.

Aunt Jack became increasingly active in the church and in 1970 moved to Hooper, Alabama. There she joined the church at Berney Points, where the Reverend Bill Greason, formerly of the Birmingham Black Barons, was pastor. Aunt Jack started a mentoring program for young women, which she maintained for over fifteen years.

Biddy's parents, Macon and Janie Owens, continued to live in Birmingham. Both became active in the civil rights movement of the sixties, Macon working through his church to increase voter registration. Both Macon and Janie also worked with a relief organization for those people injured or put out of work during the protest movements.

Biddy Owens started at Talladega College in Talladega, Alabama, two weeks after what turned out to be the last Negro League World Series. He coached the Talladega baseball team for the four years he attended school as a business major. After graduating he worked in the purchasing department at Miles College in Birmingham and, later, for the Birmingham office of the North Carolina Mutual Insurance Company. He married the former Jasmine Hinton. They have three children: two sons who teach in Birmingham and a daughter who is a sportscaster for a news conglomerate in Atlanta, Georgia. Biddy is now retired and is working to expand the Little League baseball program in Birmingham.

Life in America
in 1948

Historical Note

Baseball has been played in America, by whites and blacks, since long before the Civil War. In the years of peace after the war, baseball grew and in 1884, Moses Fleetwood Walker became the first black man to play in an organized major league when he signed with a team in Toledo, Ohio. His brother, Welday Walker, also played briefly for Toledo. But racial attitudes were such that these black players were soon banned from organized baseball. It was not until the signing of Jackie Robinson some sixty-two years later that America's favorite game was again openly integrated.

In response to the segregation practices, black players began to form their own leagues. Many of these leagues were made up of company teams. Some played against white minor-league teams, while others played only against black teams. In 1920, Andrew "Rube" Foster, a black baseball player and team owner, organized the Negro National League. This league attracted the best black ballplayers in the country. They played with the same rules as the white leagues, but the teams often struggled just to remain financially viable. Few black teams had their own stadiums, and were sometimes forced to play on open fields, hoping to attract whatever fans they could. After the game the teams' managers would pass the hat, hoping to make enough money to pay the players.

As white baseball prospered and became the national pastime, the Negro National League, under the guidance of Foster, also began to prosper. The white leagues had such legendary players as Babe Ruth, Ty Cobb, Walter Johnson, and Lou Gehrig. The Negro Leagues had Oscar Charleston, Rube Foster, Satchel Paige, Martin Dihigo, Buck Leonard, and Josh Gibson.

How good were the black players? Since the records of the white major leaguers are the standard of excellence, and they never played official league games against Negro teams, it is hard to make a direct comparison between the two leagues. In the 1930s and early 1940s, white major leaguers, in the off season, would often travel with an All-Star team and play against black All-Stars. In these games the black players did well, winning as many games as they lost. Records of the Negro Leagues are scant and often inaccurate. Few newspapers covered the games. Even black newspapers would cover only home games, and rarely printed box scores. But the truest barometer of the skills of the Negro League players came when the major leagues began to accept black players. Their play against white major leaguers left no doubt as to their ability.

The 1948 Birmingham Black Barons played a total of seventy-six regular season league games. In between the league games they played nonleague games, sometimes as many as three games in a day. In one day they might face a professional pitcher, destined to move on to the major leagues, in a day game, and then face an amateur pitcher in a night contest. It was not unusual for teams to travel hundreds of miles at night and arrive at a ball field with just enough time to change into their uniforms and run out onto the field.

One of the highlights of the season for black baseball was the East-West All-Star game, an annual event starting in 1933, usually held in Chicago's Comiskey Park. These games, as well as many of the league games, often attracted a larger attendance than white major-league games.

In 1937 the Negro American League was formed. This set up the possibility of a Negro American League and Negro National League World Series. By this time, all baseball fans knew about the Negro League stars. Fans, both white and black, would travel miles to see the legendary Satchel Paige or the daring base running of Cool Papa Bell. But major-league owners still resisted the integration of baseball. There was never an official rule that major-league teams could not hire a black player, but it was understood that no one would.

During World War II baseball suffered from a lack of available players. Black organizations such as the N.A.A.C.P. (National Association for the Advancement of Colored People) asked why, if blacks in the army could throw grenades for America in wartime, they couldn't throw baseballs in peacetime?

When the war ended, baseball attendance for white teams was down. Many of the black teams were drawing larger crowds than their white counterparts. The Negro Leagues often rented the same fields used by white major leaguers. So when Josh Gibson hit one of his mighty shots into the bleachers at Comiskey Park, it could be measured against the hits that Babe Ruth hit in the same park. When a black outfielder threw a runner out, the distances were easily measured. Many fans thought that some of the Negro League teams, such as the Kansas City Monarchs, the Birmingham Black Barons, or the Homestead Grays, could have competed in either white major league.

Branch Rickey, president of the Brooklyn Dodgers organization, understood that major-league baseball would eventually be forced to accept black players. He began looking at the Negro Leagues for potential players for the

Dodgers. On October 23, 1945, the Dodgers announced that a Negro player, Jack Roosevelt (Jackie) Robinson, had been signed to play for their farm club, the Montreal Royals. As predicted, many southerners objected to the hiring of a black in the all-white world of major-league ball. Other baseball fans, white and black, knew it was about time.

Robinson's selection had been carefully thought out by Rickey. Robinson, who had been a football and track star at U.C.L.A. before the war, was a conservative, well-spoken man. His older brother, Mack, had been a silver medalist in the 1936 Olympics. Robinson had also been an officer in the U.S. Army during the war. He had only played one season for the Kansas City Monarchs in the Negro Leagues and was not considered an outstanding player according to Negro Leagues standards. But Rickey had assessed that Robinson could withstand the racism he would face and would handle himself well if he encountered racial problems. In other words, he would represent his race well.

Another reason for selecting Robinson for the Dodgers was that the Dodger farm club played in Montreal, Canada, where there was no segregation. Robinson went to Montreal in 1946 and became the first black player of the century in the major leagues in April 1947. Robinson did receive the taunts of racist players and fans, but Rickey had been right: He was able to handle the pressure and had an outstanding rookie season. Larry Doby, of the Newark Eagles, was taken on by the Cleveland Indians in July 1947, and Hank Thompson, also from the Kansas City team, was called up by the St. Louis Browns.

By the end of the 1948 season the white major-league teams had staged an onslaught on the Negro Leagues. They took the players they wanted, signing the stars they had shunned for years and assigning them to either major-league teams or to their farm clubs in the minors.

Black fans wanted to see how the players from the Negro Leagues did against the white stars. Attendance at Negro League games began to drop drastically in 1948. The sports pages of black newspapers would headline what Jackie Robinson and Roy Campanella, who had played for the Baltimore Elite Giants, were doing. Negro League games received less and less coverage as interest waned in favor of integrated baseball. Another blow was the growth of television. In 1948, baseball fans could, for the first time, sit in the comfort of their own homes and see major-league stars. The result was that the 1948 League World Series between the Birmingham Black Barons and the Homestead Grays was the last ever played in the Negro Leagues.

Four players from the 1948 Barons eventually played

in the major leagues. Jehosie Heard played briefly with the Baltimore Orioles, and Bill Greason played with the St. Louis Cardinals. Artie Wilson and Willie Mays played with the New York Giants. In 1979, Willie Mays was elected to the Baseball Hall of Fame.

Few people remember the old Negro Leagues, or the days of segregated seating at the stadiums. Baseball has grown to be a huge business with players making salaries early ballplayers could scarcely imagine. There are only a few of the old Negro League players still alive to tell the stories of their glory days and to remind us of how things used to be. Today, no one is barred from the major leagues because of the color of their skin. Anyone who can consistently hit a ball thrown at nearly one hundred miles an hour, or who can throw it at that speed, or who can run down the hard-hit ball that threatens to win a game, can compete for a chance in professional baseball. The game is better for it.

BASEBALL

Birmingham Black Barons

vs.

House of David

COVINGTON PARK

WEDNESDAY NIGHT

JULY 8 . . . 7 P.M.

Although there was a brief period of time in the late 1800s when blacks were allowed to play in baseball's major leagues, racial unrest in America soon led to a ban on interracial activities. The Negro Leagues resulted from that tragic time in America's history. The Negro League teams faced awful hardships along the way but changed the face and spirit of baseball as they played against other league teams or in pick-up games on any field they could find. They challenged the country and one another to step up to the plate. Here, a poster announces a Negro League game.

Perhaps the most obvious racism came in the form of enforced segregation. From drinking fountains (above) to waiting rooms (below), players in the Negro Leagues would never forget that they were still considered second-class citizens. Discrimination made traveling a real trial for the teams, who spent many meals and many nights aboard their buses.

The legendary Rickwood Field was the site used by the Birmingham Black Barons. Every other Sunday, when the "white" Barons were out of town, people would line up for a game to see the stars of the League in action.

The Negro League teams traveled to all of their games on buses like this one belonging to the Birmingham Black Barons.

The Negro League games brought crowds of black fans to the stands. Pride in having teams and players of their own color was important to the unity of the black community. In fact, many of the black teams drew more people than the white teams of the time.

In addition to their seventy-six regular season league games, the 1948 Birmingham Black Barons played non-league games against college, industrial, and pick-up teams. Some days they played as many as three games.

Ed Steele, Piper Davis, and Art Wilson (left to right) were players on the 1948 Birmingham Black Barons.

— SOUVENIR —
1st Negro World Series
YANKEE STADIUM
1942

*The Great
Satchell Paige*

Pitcher Leroy Robert "Satchell" Paige's showmanship and skill made him one of the most celebrated Negro League players.

Willie Mays was one of the players from the 1948 Black Barons who went on to great success in the major leagues with the New York Giants. In 1979, he was inducted into the Baseball Hall of Fame.

Although Negro League players were not usually recognized by the major leagues, their accomplishments matched those of some of the most talented white players. Indeed, a Josh Gibson hit might as well have been a Babe Ruth hit, as they often played the same venues as their white counterparts.

Perhaps the most famous and beloved player to emerge from the Negro Leagues was Jackie Robinson. His signing with the Brooklyn Dodgers made history. However, while it broke the color barrier in baseball and opened the door for Robinson's peers, it also marked the beginning of the end for the Negro Leagues.

This 1945 photo, taken at Griffith Stadium in Washington, D.C., shows Walter Fenner "Buck" Leonard of the Homestead Grays trying to beat out a throw to Leonard Pearson of the Newark Eagles.

Among the factors that contibuted to the end of the Negro League era were the focus of the fans on the players that had integrated major league baseball, and the fact that games could now be watched on television. Subsequent low attendance at Negro League games made the triumphant victory of the Black Barons at their League Championship their last. Indeed, the 1948 Negro Leagues World Series, which the Black Barons lost, was the grand finale to an era of defining moments in American sports and social history.

This modern map shows the location of Birmingham, Alabama.

About the Author

Walter Dean Myers saw his first baseball game at the old Ebbets Field in Brooklyn, New York. A Brooklyn Dodgers fan even before the arrival of Jackie Robinson, and a really sore loser, he spent many hours in ardent prayer on behalf of his beloved Bums. When the Dodgers moved to Los Angeles he shifted his loyalty to the New York Yankees.

Walter played sandlot baseball in Harlem and the Bronx as a teenager. In his prime he was an outstanding outfielder but, sadly, couldn't hit for two cents.

Walter Dean Myers is an award-winning writer of fiction, nonfiction, and poetry for young people. His other books for the My Name Is America series are *The Journal of Scott Pendleton Collins, A World War II Soldier* and *The Journal of Joshua Loper, A Black Cowboy*. Most recently, for *Monster* (HarperCollins), Myers won the Michael L. Printz Award, which honors the highest literary achievement in books for young adults. Myers's other books for Scholastic include *The Greatest: Muhammad Ali; Harlem*, which was illustrated by his son Christopher Myers and was named a Caldecott Honor book; *Slam!; Somewhere in the Darkness; Fallen Angels,* winner of the Coretta Scott King Award; *Malcolm X; By Any Means Necessary,* a Coretta Scott King Honor Book and ALA Notable Children's Book; and *The Glory Field,* an ALA Best Book for Young Adults and a Notable Children's Trade Book in the Field of Social Studies. Mr. Myers is the recipient of two awards for the body of his work: the Margaret A. Edwards Award for Outstanding Literature for Young Adults and the ALAN Award. He lives in Jersey City, New Jersey.

Acknowledgments

The author would like to thank David Brewer, Director, Friends of Rickwood, for his help in preparing this manuscript.

Grateful acknowledgment is made for permission to reprint the following:

Cover portrait: Jimmy Newberry. Courtesy of the T.H. Hayes Collection, Memphis Shelby Public Library, Memphis, Tennessee. Cover background: 1948 Birmingham Black Barons team picture. Courtesy of the National Baseball Hall of Fame Library, Cooperstown, New York.

Foldout map illustration by Bryn Barnard.

Page 126: Announcement. Courtesy of the National Baseball Hall of Fame Library, Cooperstown, New York.

Page 127 (top): Segregated drinking fountain in use in the American South. Corbis-Bettman, New York.

Page 127 (bottom): Segregated bus station in the South. Library of Congress/Jack Delano.

Page 128 (top): Black Barons fans in line for a game at Rickwood Field. Courtesy of the T.H. Hayes Collection, Memphis Shelby Public Library, Memphis, Tennessee.

Page 128 (bottom): Birmingham Black Barons team bus. Courtesy of the T.H. Hayes Collection, Memphis Shelby Public Library, Memphis, Tennessee.

Page 129: Fans at Homestead Grays game. Courtesy of the National Baseball Hall of Fame Library, Cooperstown, New York.

Page 130 (top): 1948 Birmingham Black Barons team picture. Courtesy of the National Baseball Hall of Fame Library, Cooperstown, New York.

Page 130 (bottom): Ed Steele, Piper Davis, and Art Wilson. Courtesy of the National Baseball Hall of Fame, Cooperstown, New York.

Page 131: Leroy "Satchel" Paige, 1942. Courtesy of the Schomburg Center for Research in Black Culture, New York, New York.

Page 132: Willie Mays, 1950. Courtesy of the T.H. Hayes Collection, Memphis Shelby Public Library, Memphis, Tennessee.

Page 133: Josh Gibson. Courtesy of the National Baseball Hall of Fame Library, Cooperstown, New York.

Page 134 (top): Stealing home. Corbis-Bettman, New York.

Page 134 (bottom): Buck Leonard. Courtesy of the National Baseball Hall of Fame Library, Cooperstown, New York.

Page 135 (top): Celebration of team championship. Courtesy of the Negro League Baseball Museum, Kansas City, Missouri.

Page 135 (bottom): Map by Heather Saunders.

Other books in the My Name Is America series

The Journal of William Thomas Emerson
A Revolutionary War Patriot
by Barry Denenberg

The Journal of James Edmond Pease
A Civil War Union Soldier
by Jim Murphy

The Journal of Joshua Loper
A Black Cowboy
by Walter Dean Myers

The Journal of Scott Pendleton Collins
A World War II Soldier
by Walter Dean Myers

The Journal of Sean Sullivan
A Transcontinental Railroad Worker
by William Durbin

For David Key, III, for whom the players in the Negro Leagues are a distant, but glorious, history

While the events described and some of the characters in this book may be based on actual historical events and real people, Biddy Owens is a fictional character, created by the author, and his journal and its epilogue are works of fiction.

Library of Congress Cataloging-in-Publication Data
Myers, Walter Dean, 1937-
  The journal of Biddy Owens, the Negro leagues / by Walter Dean Myers.
    p. cm.—(My name is America)
  Summary: Teenager Biddy Owens' 1948 journal about working for the Birmingham Black Barons includes the games and the players, racism the team faces from New Orleans to Chicago, and his family's resistance to his becoming a professional baseball player. Includes a historical note about the evolution of the Negro Leagues.
    1. Birmingham Black Barons (Baseball team)—Juvenile fiction. 2. Afro-Americans—Juvenile fiction. [1. Birmingham Black Barons (Baseball team)—Fiction. 2. Baseball—Fiction. 3. Negro Leagues—Fiction. 4. Afro-Americans—Fiction. 5. Segregation—Fiction. 6. Prejudices—Fiction. 7. Diaries—Fiction.] I. Title. II. Series.

PZ7.M992 Ji 2001
[Fic]—dc21

00-044667

ISBN (paper over board) 0-439-09503-4

10 9 8 7 6 5 4 3 2 1   01 02 03 04 05

The display type was set in Merz Irregular
The text type was set in Berling Roman
Book design by Elizabeth B. Parisi
Photo research by Zoe Moffitt

Printed in the U.S.A. 23
First edition, April 2001